BENJAMIN BEAR

IN

FUZZY THINKING

PHILIPPE COUDRAY

BENJAMIN BEAR

IN

FUZZY THINKING

It's *nice* to get out of the snow!
!

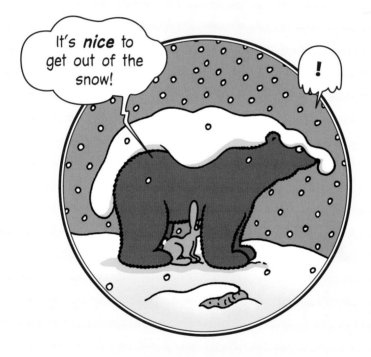

A TOON BOOK BY

PHILIPPE COUDRAY

TOON BOOKS IS AN IMPRINT OF CANDLEWICK PRESS

ABDO Spotlight

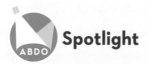

For Robert, Debbie, and their children

Editorial Director: FRANÇOISE MOULY

Book Design: FRANÇOISE MOULY & JONATHAN BENNETT

Translation: LEIGH STEIN

PHILIPPE COUDRAY'S artwork was drawn in india ink and colored digitally

ABDOPUBLISHING.COM

Reinforced library bound edition published in 2015 by Spotlight, a division of ABDO
PO Box 398166, Minneapolis, Minnesota 55439. Spotlight produces high-quality reinforced library bound editions for schools and libraries. Published by agreement with Candlewick Press.

Printed in the United States of America, North Mankato, Minnesota.
112014
012015

 THIS BOOK CONTAINS
RECYCLED MATERIALS

LIBRARY OF CONGRESS CATALOGING-IN-PUBLICATION DATA

This book was previously cataloged with the following information:

Coudray, Philippe.
Benjamin Bear in Fuzzy thinking : a TOON book / by Philippe Coudray.
    p. cm.
Summary: Although he is a very serious bear, Benjamin Bear has a funny way of doing things, like drying dishes on a rabbit's back or sharing his sweater without taking it off.
ISBN-13: 978-1-935179-12-2 (hardcover)   ISBN-10: 1-935179-12-8 (hardcover)
1. Graphic novels. [1. Graphic novels. 2. Bears--Fiction. 3. Humorous stories.] I. Title. II. Title: Fuzzy thinking.
PZ7.7.C68Be 2011
741.5'973--dc22

2011000801

ISBN 978-1-61479-299-4 (reinforced library bound edition)

Spotlight

A Division of ABDO
abdopublishing.com

A big fish

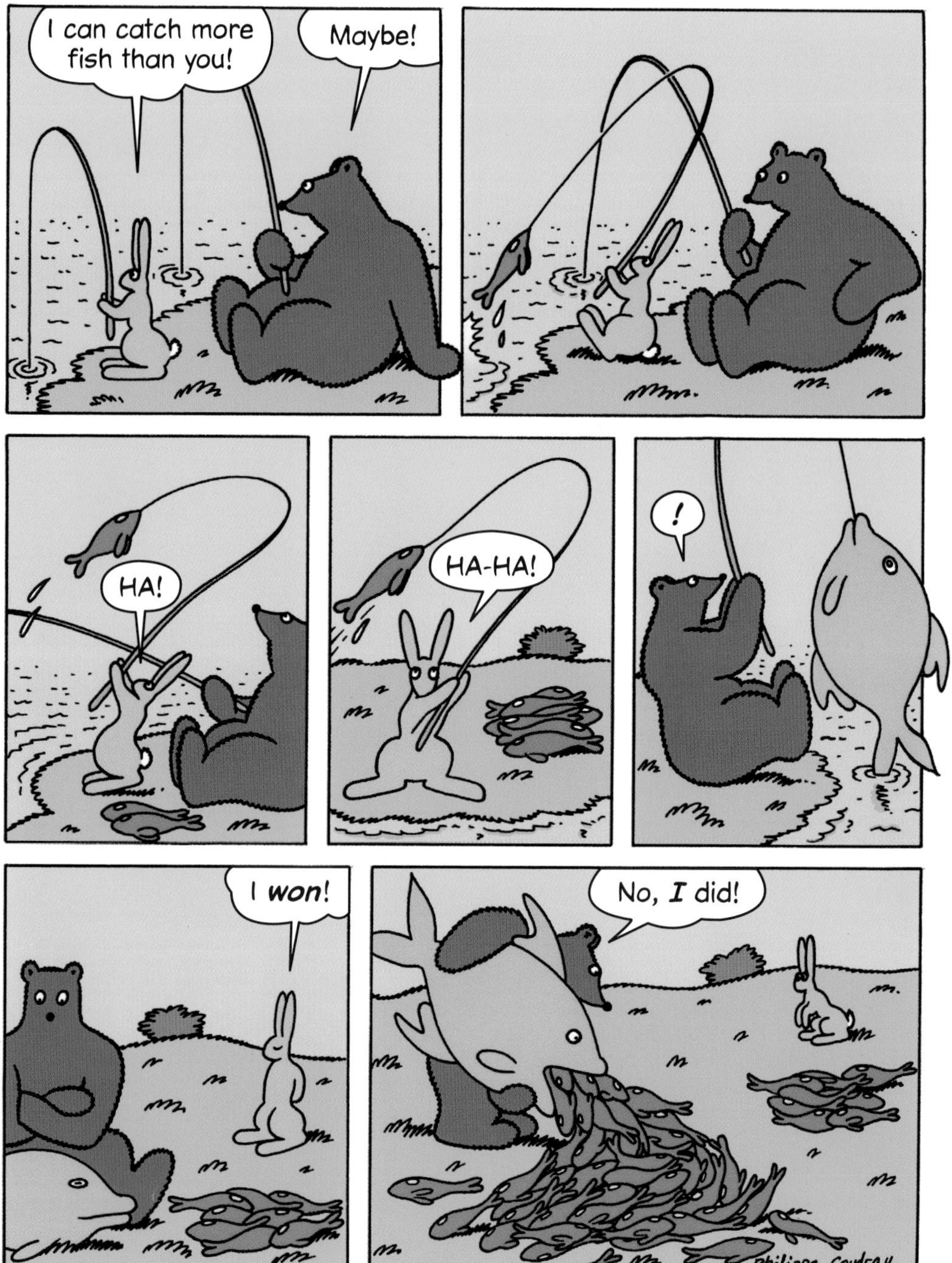
I can catch more fish than you!
Maybe!
HA!
HA-HA!
!
I *won*!
No, *I* did!
Philippe Coudray

Cold night

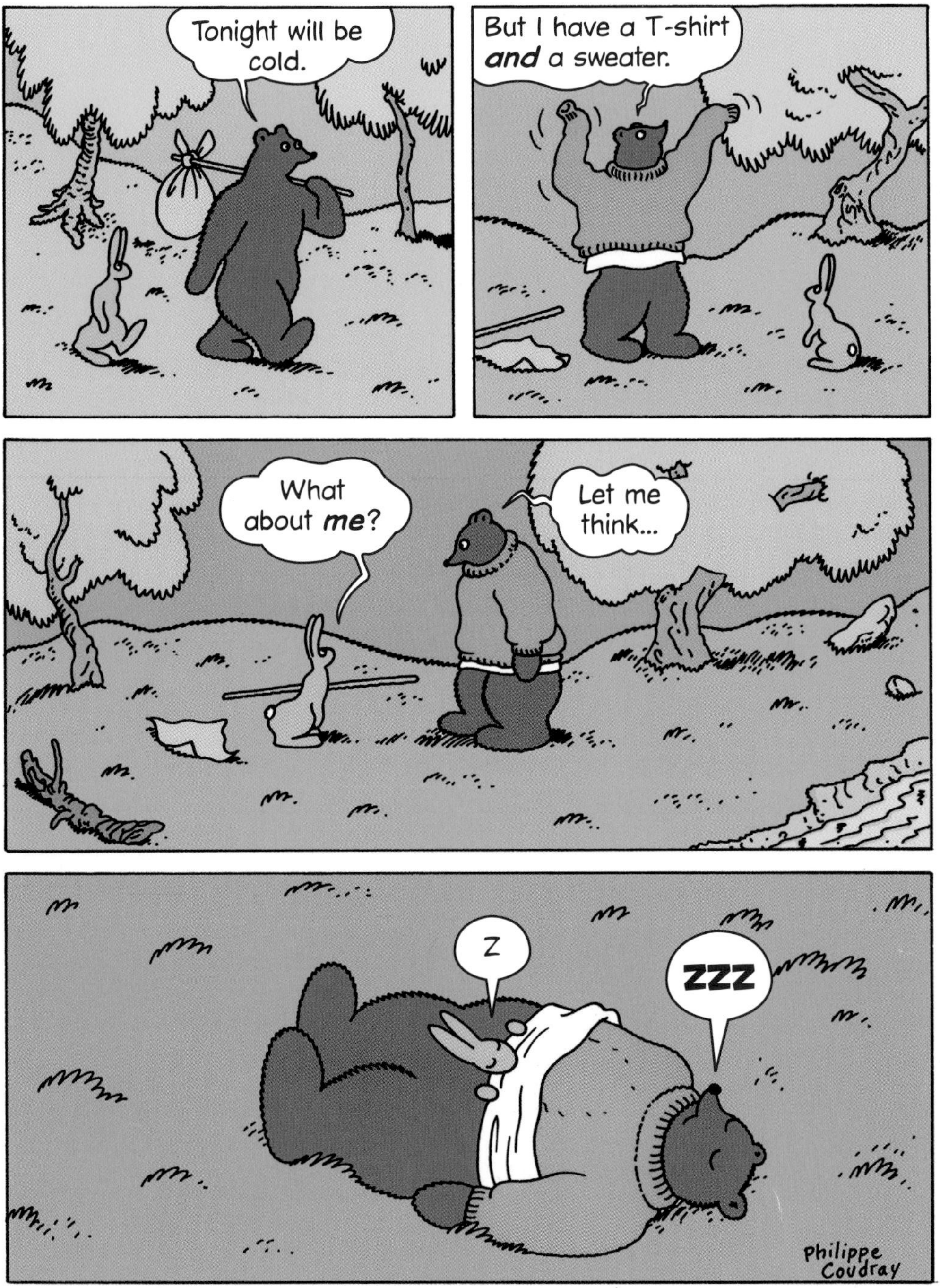
Tonight will be cold.
But I have a T-shirt *and* a sweater.
What about *me*?
Let me think...
Z
ZZZ
Philippe Coudray

Painting

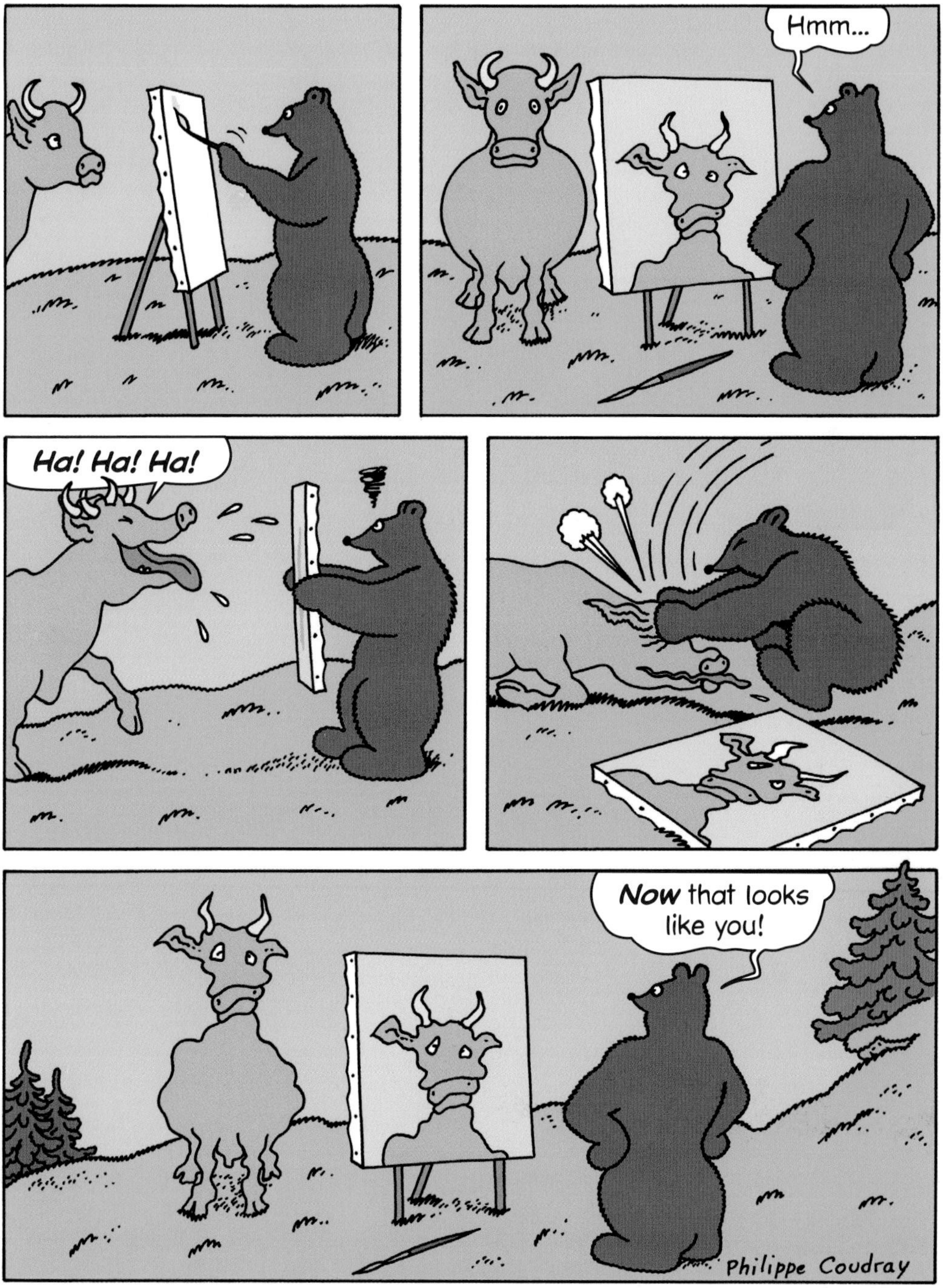
Hmm...
Ha! Ha! Ha!
Now that looks like you!
Philippe Coudray

Tall tree

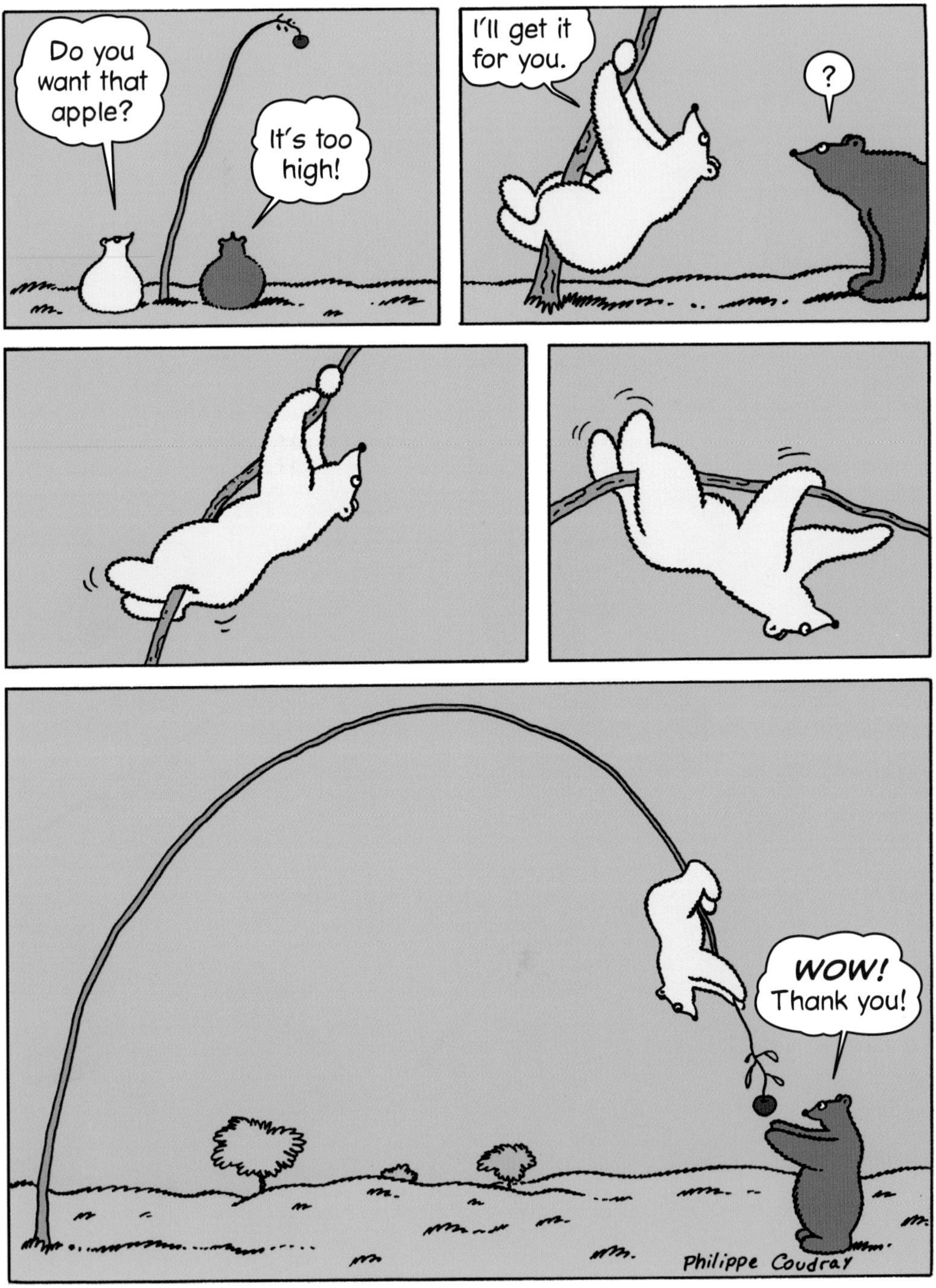
Do you want that apple?
It's too high!
I'll get it for you.
?
WOW! Thank you!
Philippe Coudray

Karate

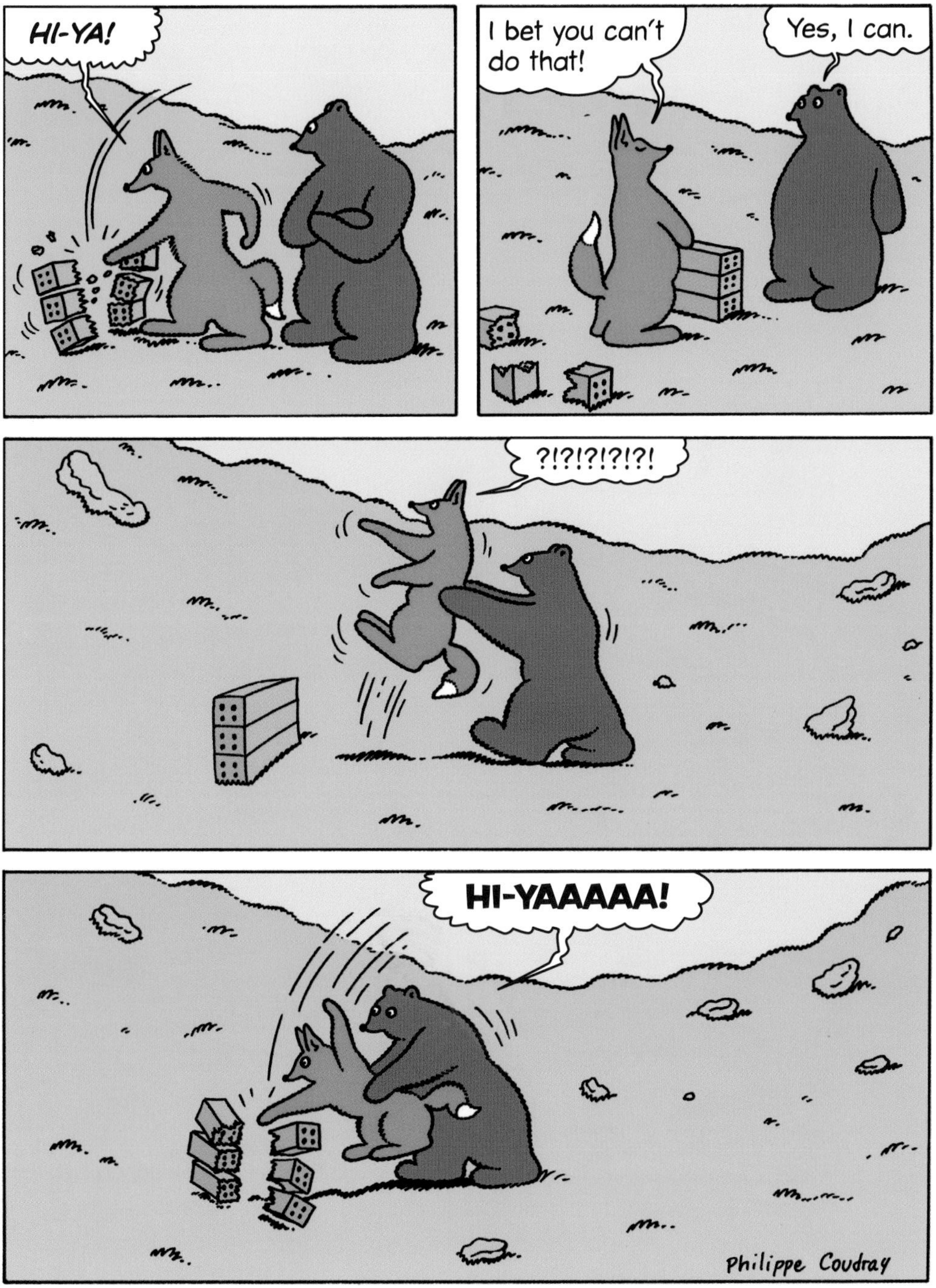
HI-YA!
I bet you can't do that!
Yes, I can.
?!?!?!?!?!
HI-YAAAAA!
Philippe Coudray

To fly—or not

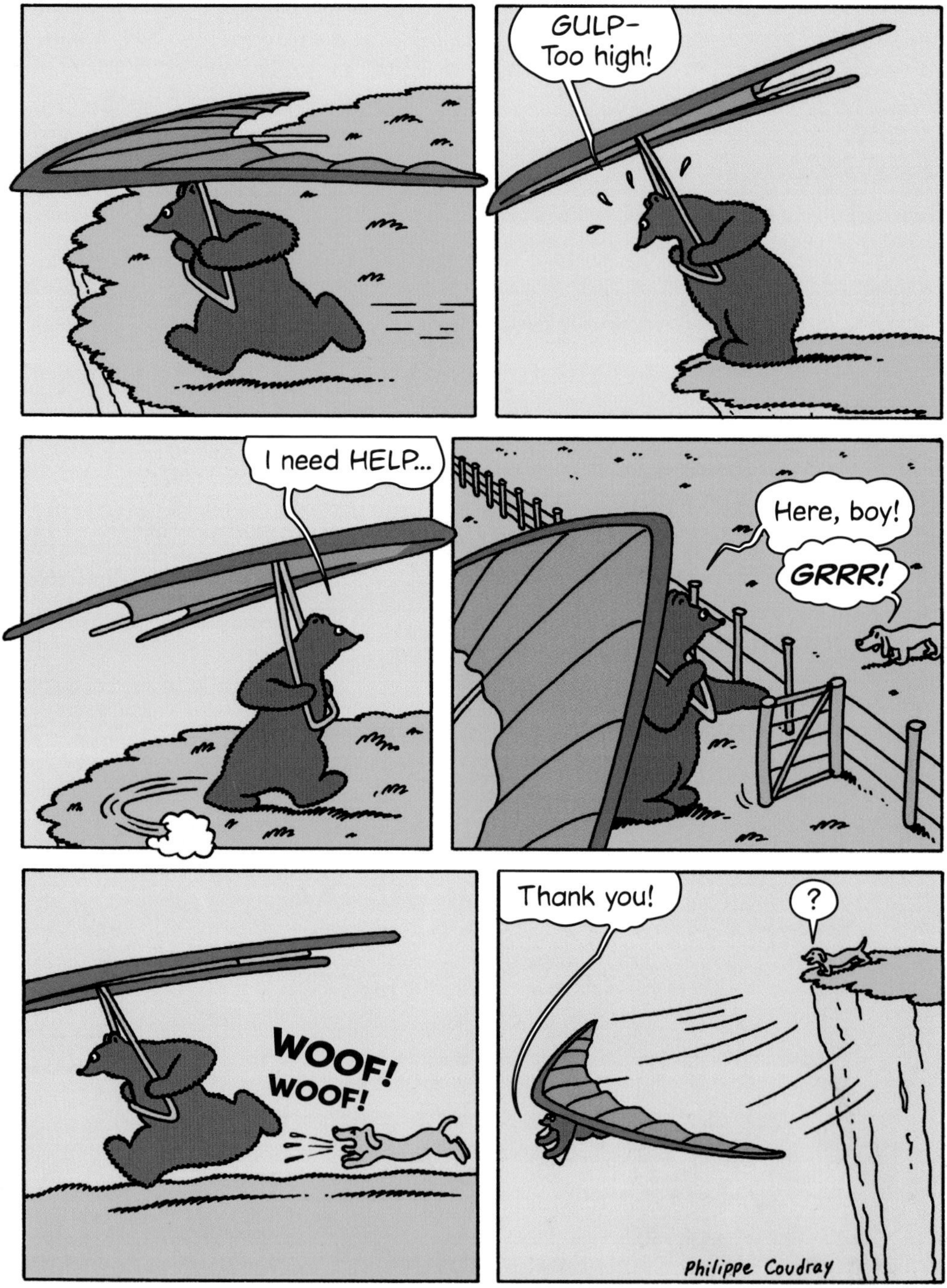
GULP-
Too high!
I need HELP...
Here, boy!
GRRR!
WOOF!
WOOF!
Thank you!
?
Philippe Coudray

A long nap

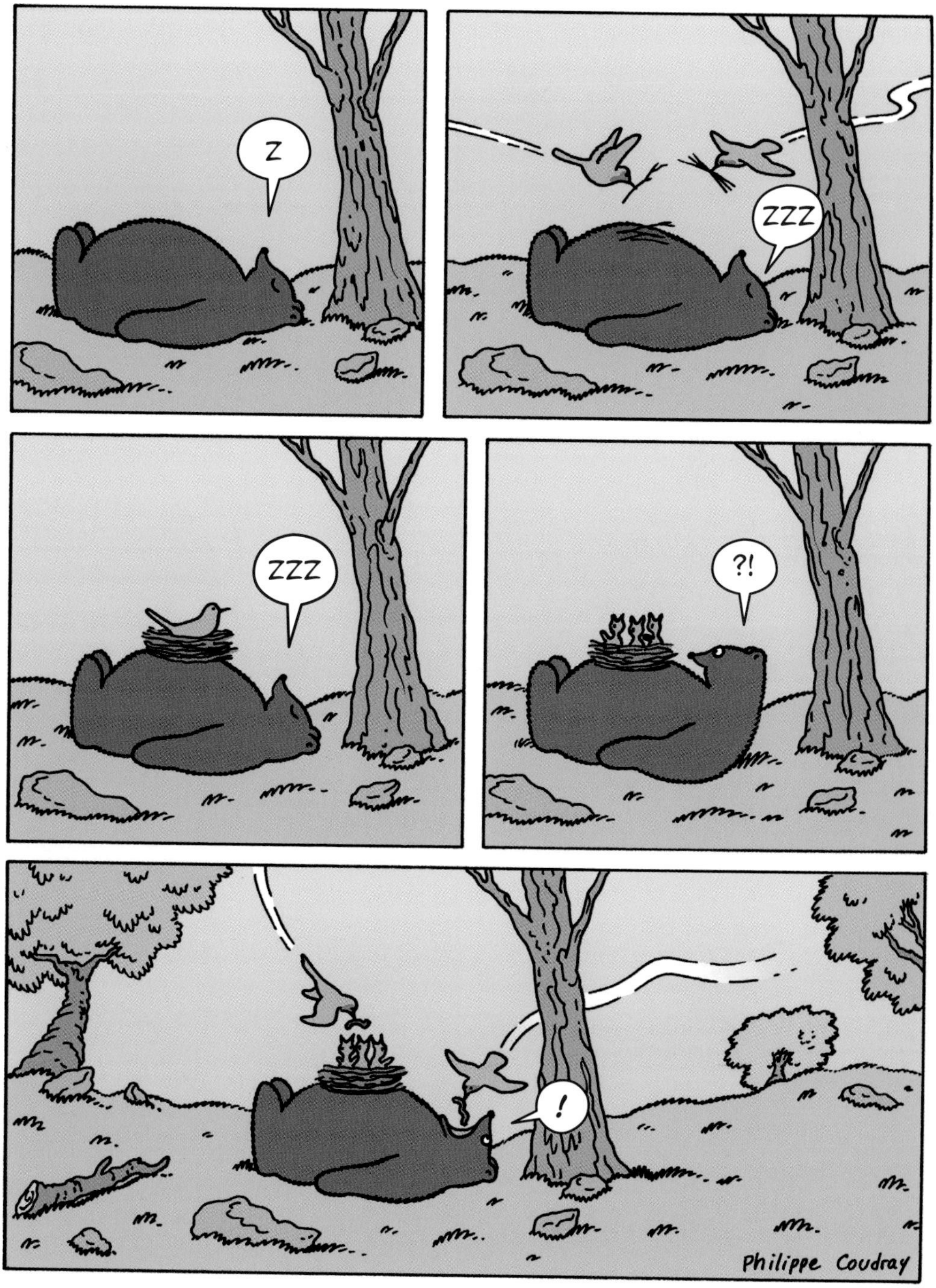

Z
ZZZ
ZZZ
?!
!
Philippe Coudray

The man in the moon

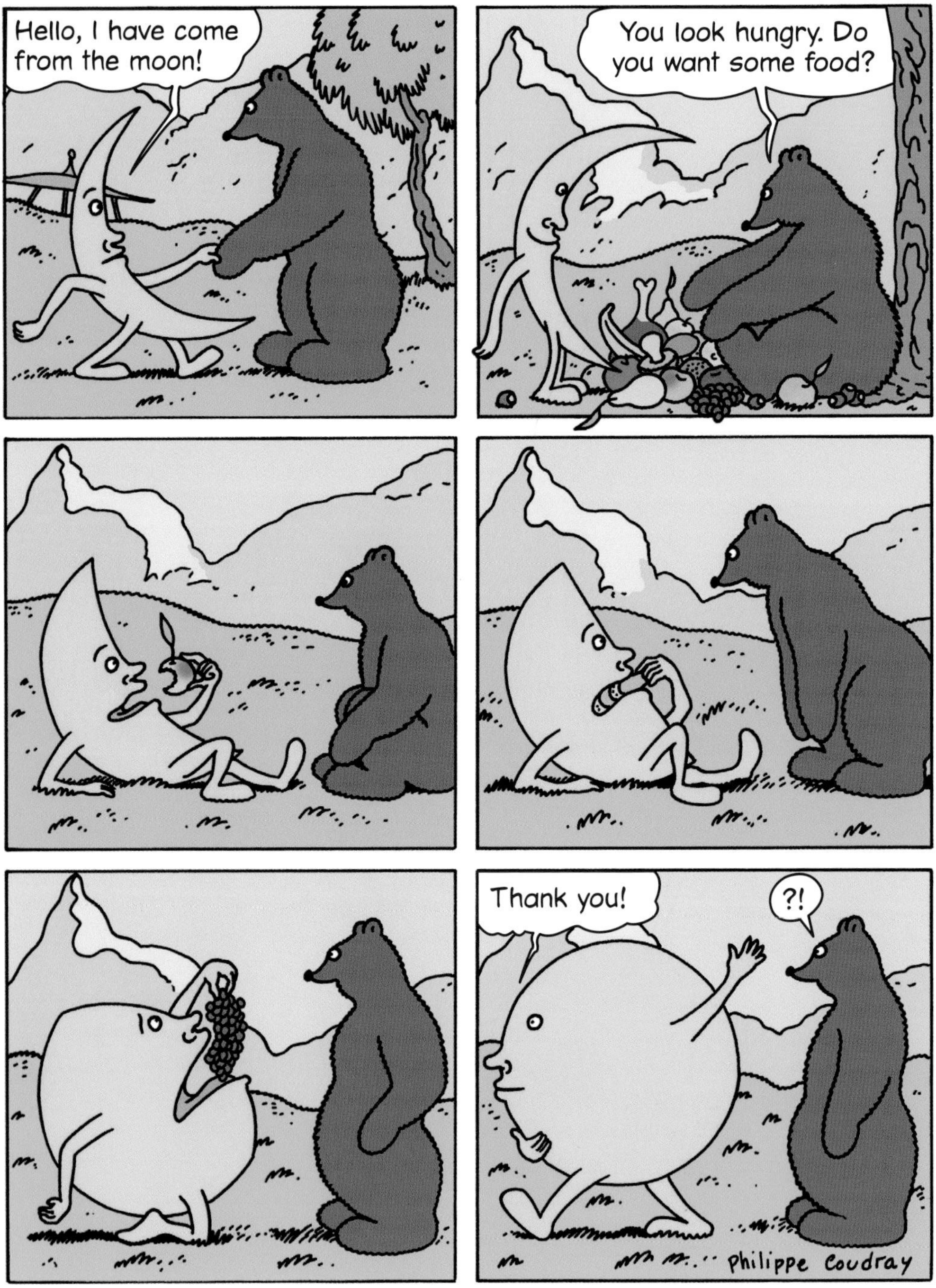

Hello, I have come from the moon!
You look hungry. Do you want some food?
Thank you!
?!
Philippe Coudray

Underwater

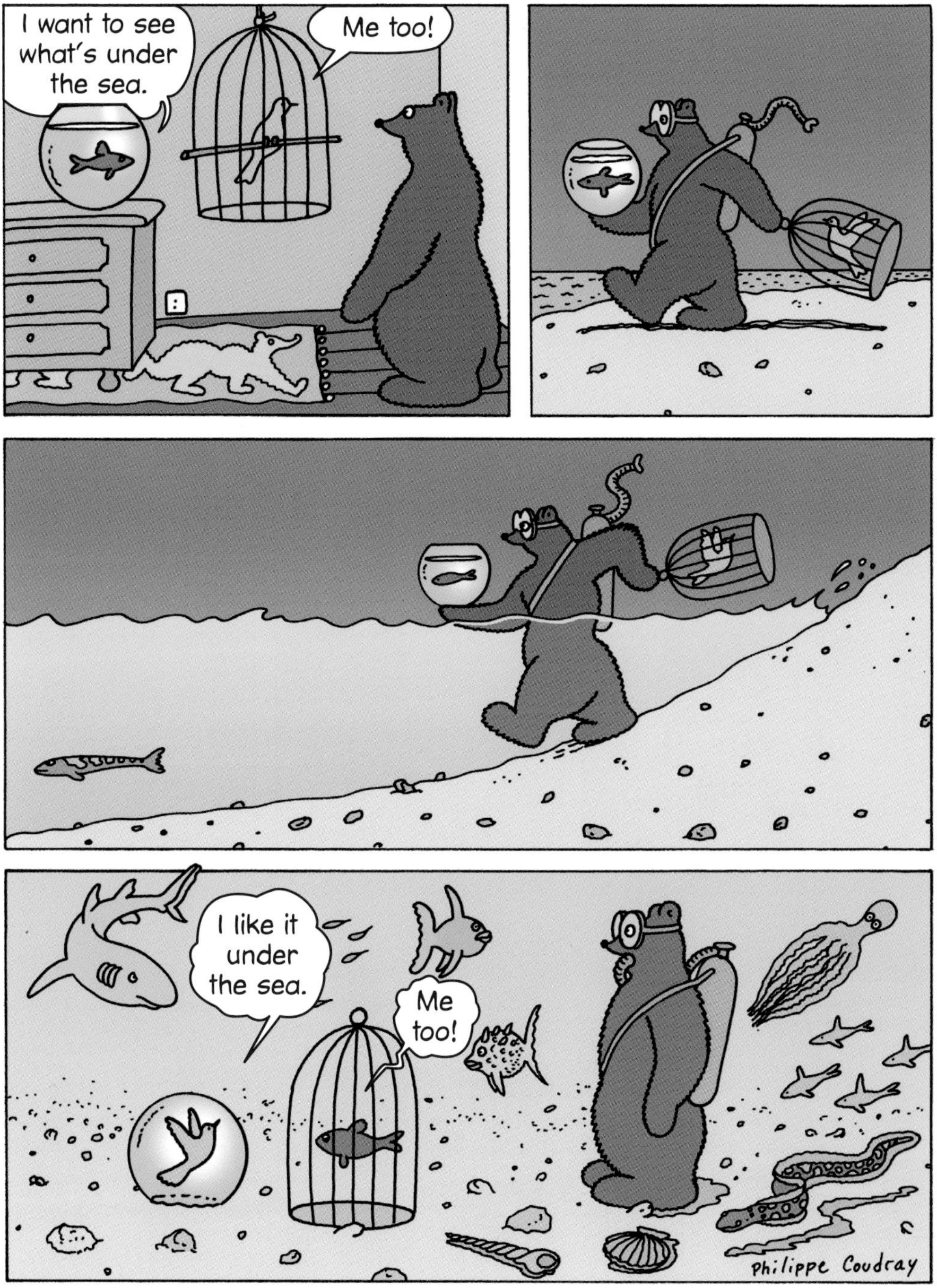
I want to see what's under the sea.
Me too!
I like it under the sea.
Me too!
Philippe Coudray

The maze

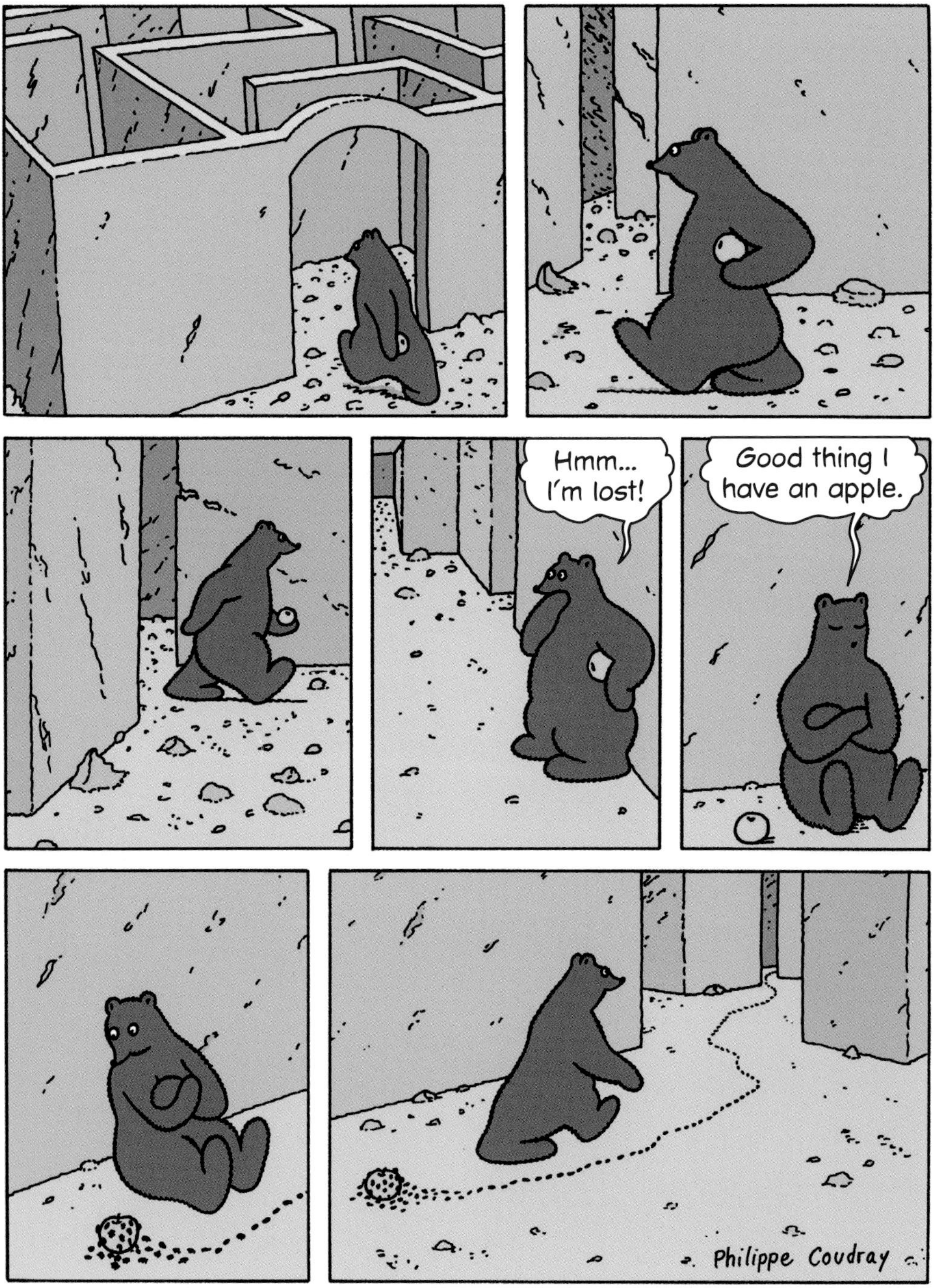

Hmm... I'm lost!
Good thing I have an apple.
Philippe Coudray

Help your friends

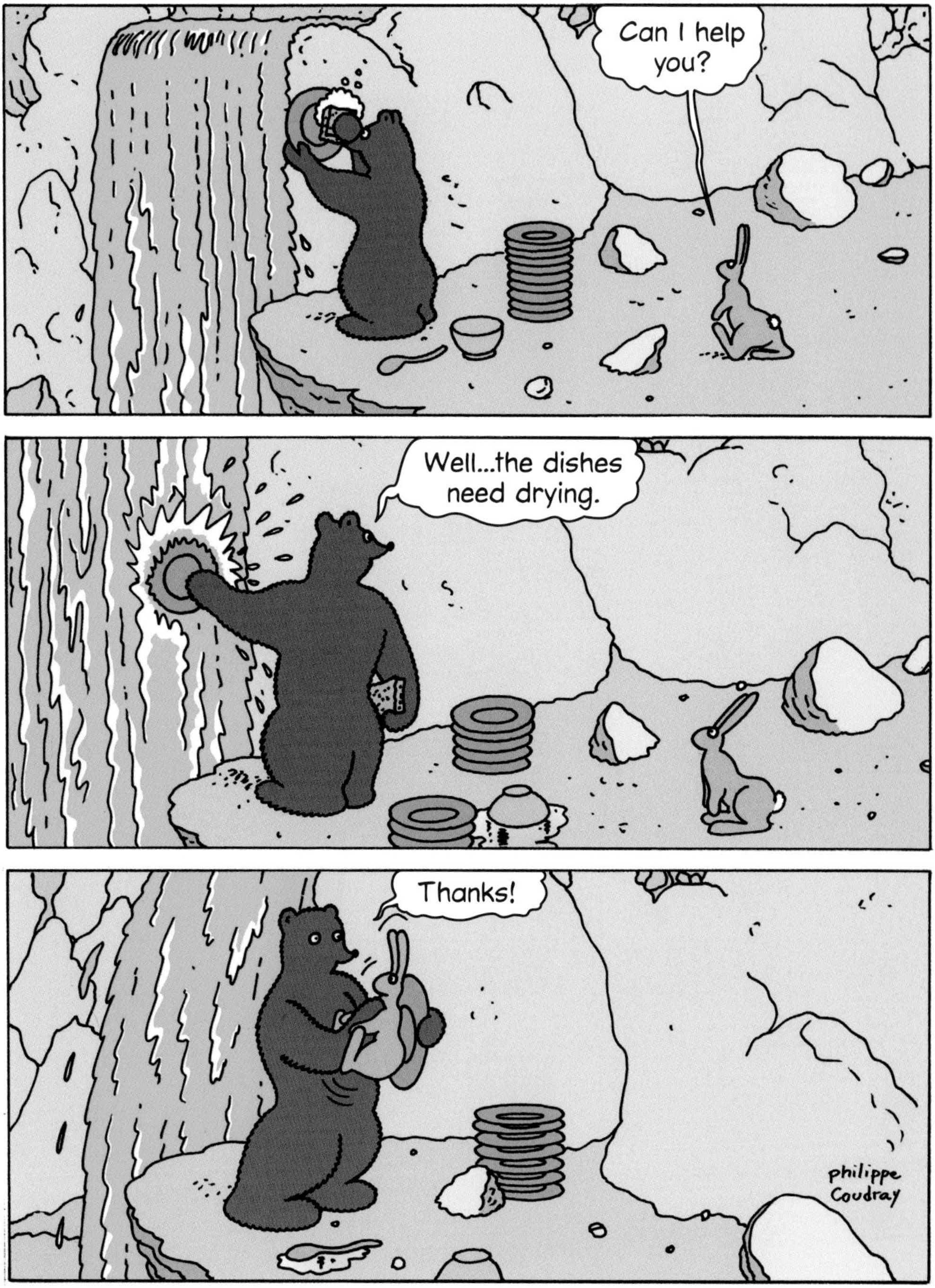
Can I help you?
Well...the dishes need drying.
Thanks!
philippe Coudray

Play with me

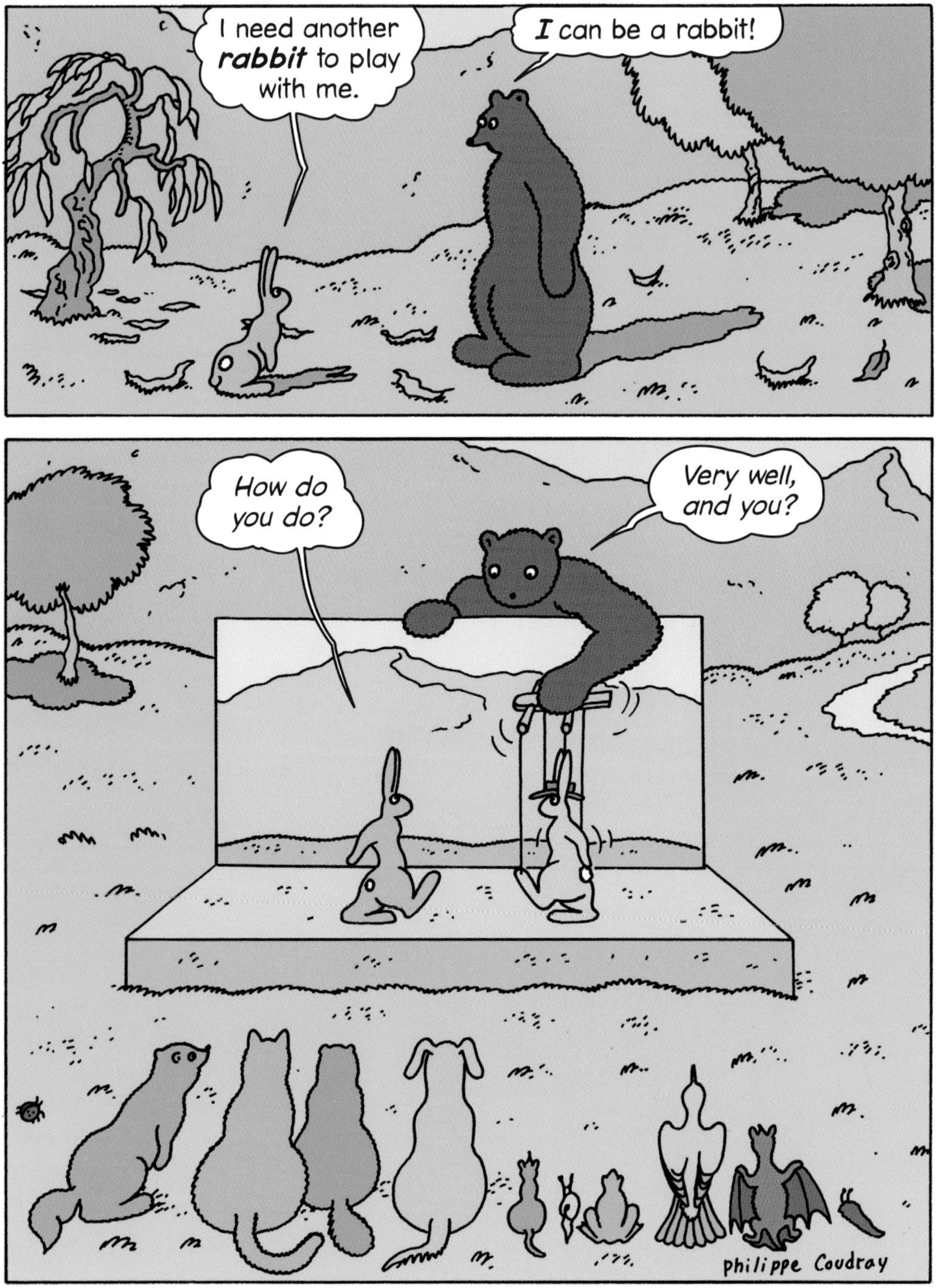

I need another **rabbit** to play with me.
I can be a rabbit!
How do you do?
Very well, and you?
Philippe Coudray

To jump—or not

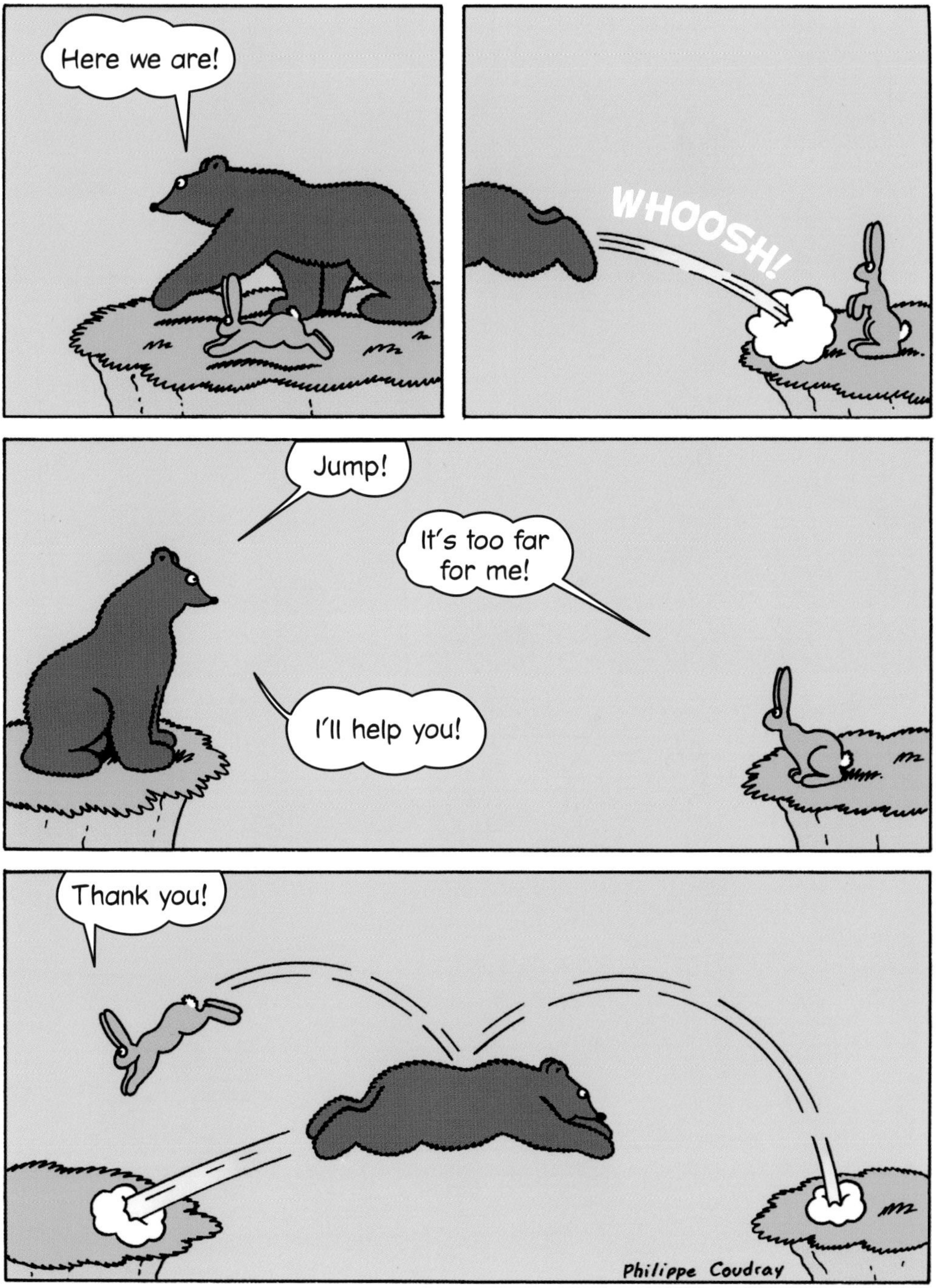
Here we are!
WHOOSH!
Jump!
It's too far for me!
I'll help you!
Thank you!
Philippe Coudray

Sailboat

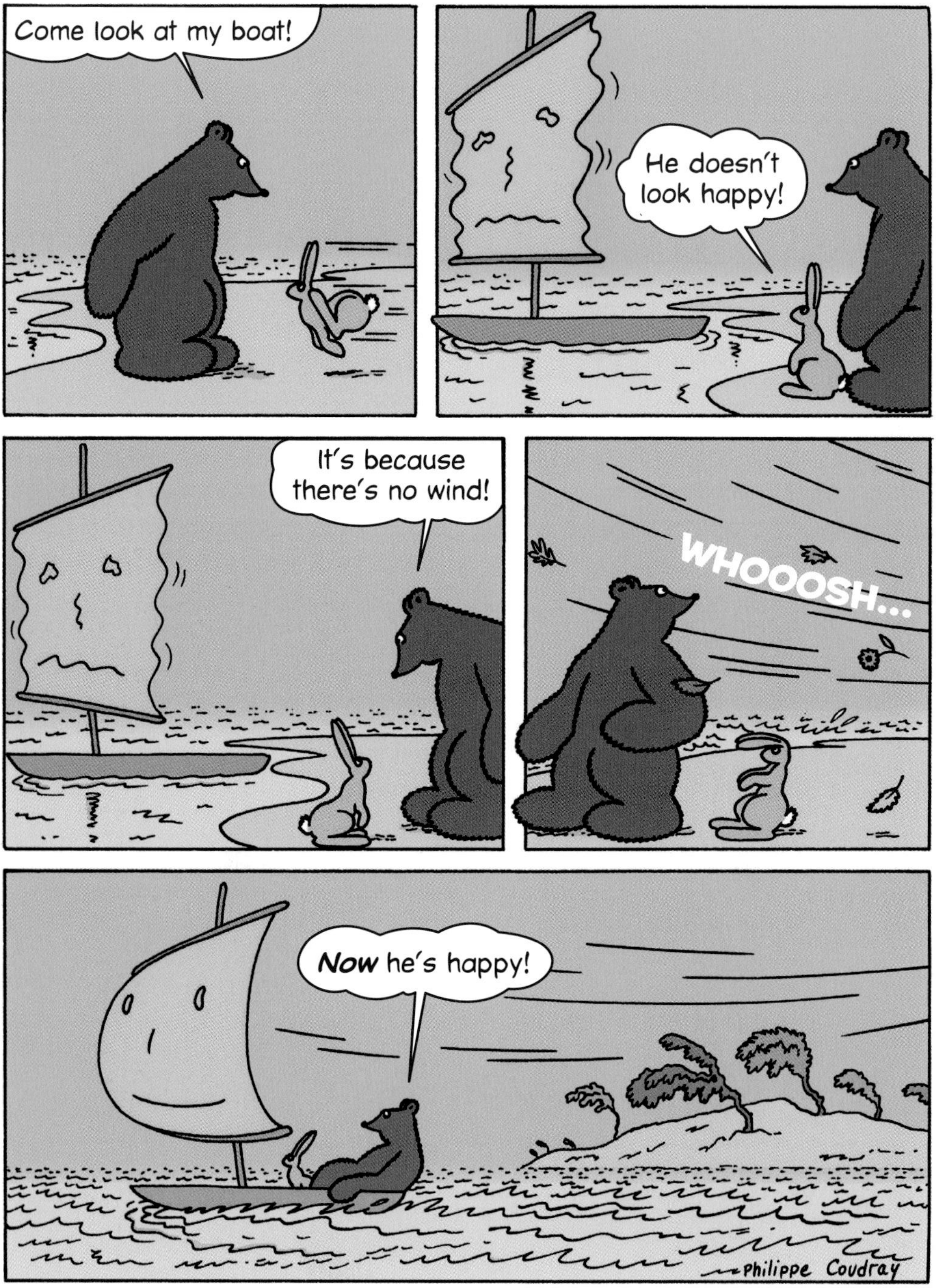
Come look at my boat!
He doesn't look happy!
It's because there's no wind!
WHOOOSH...
Now he's happy!
Philippe Coudray

At the store

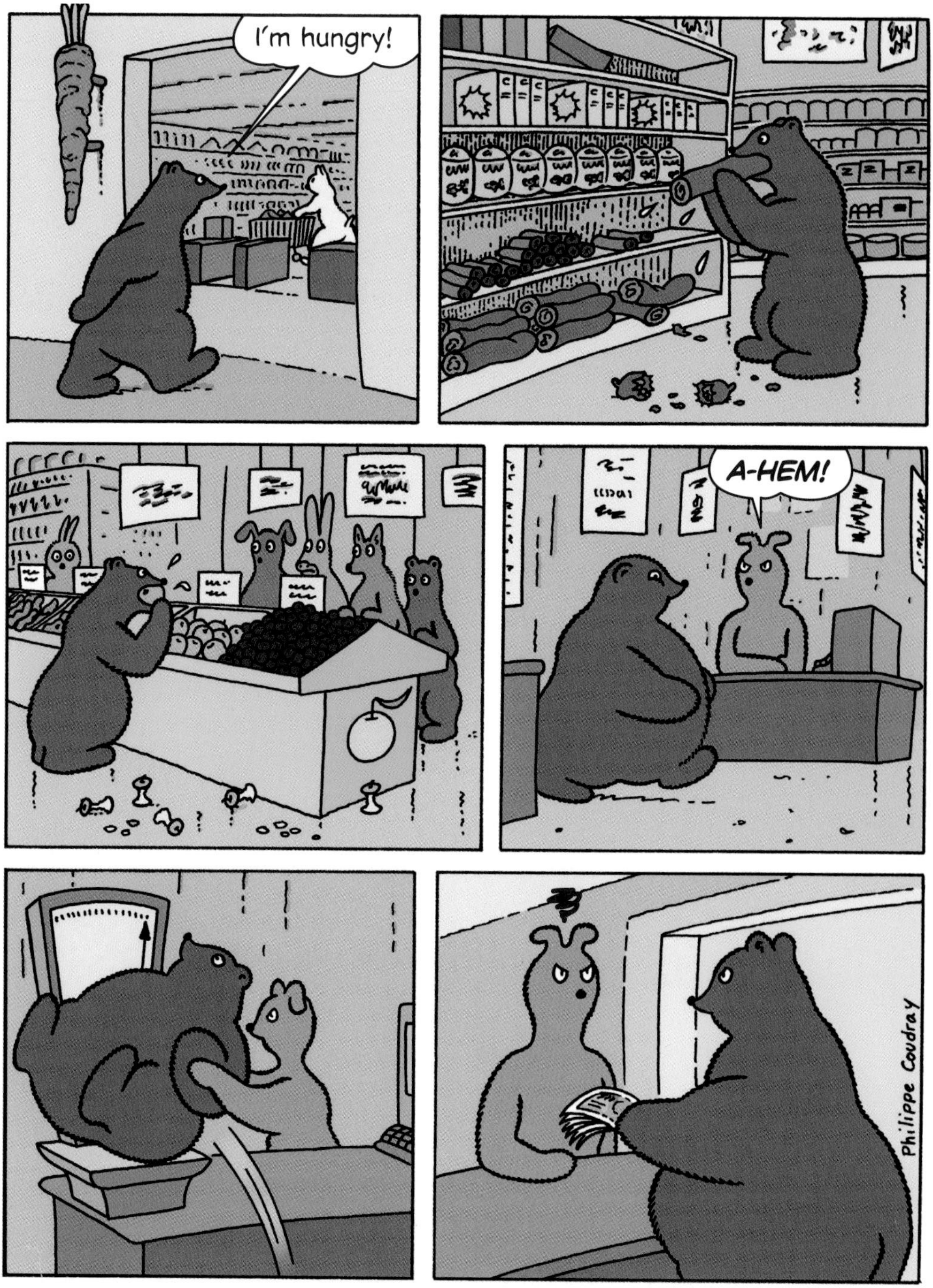
I'm hungry!
A-HEM!
Philippe Coudray

Sunset

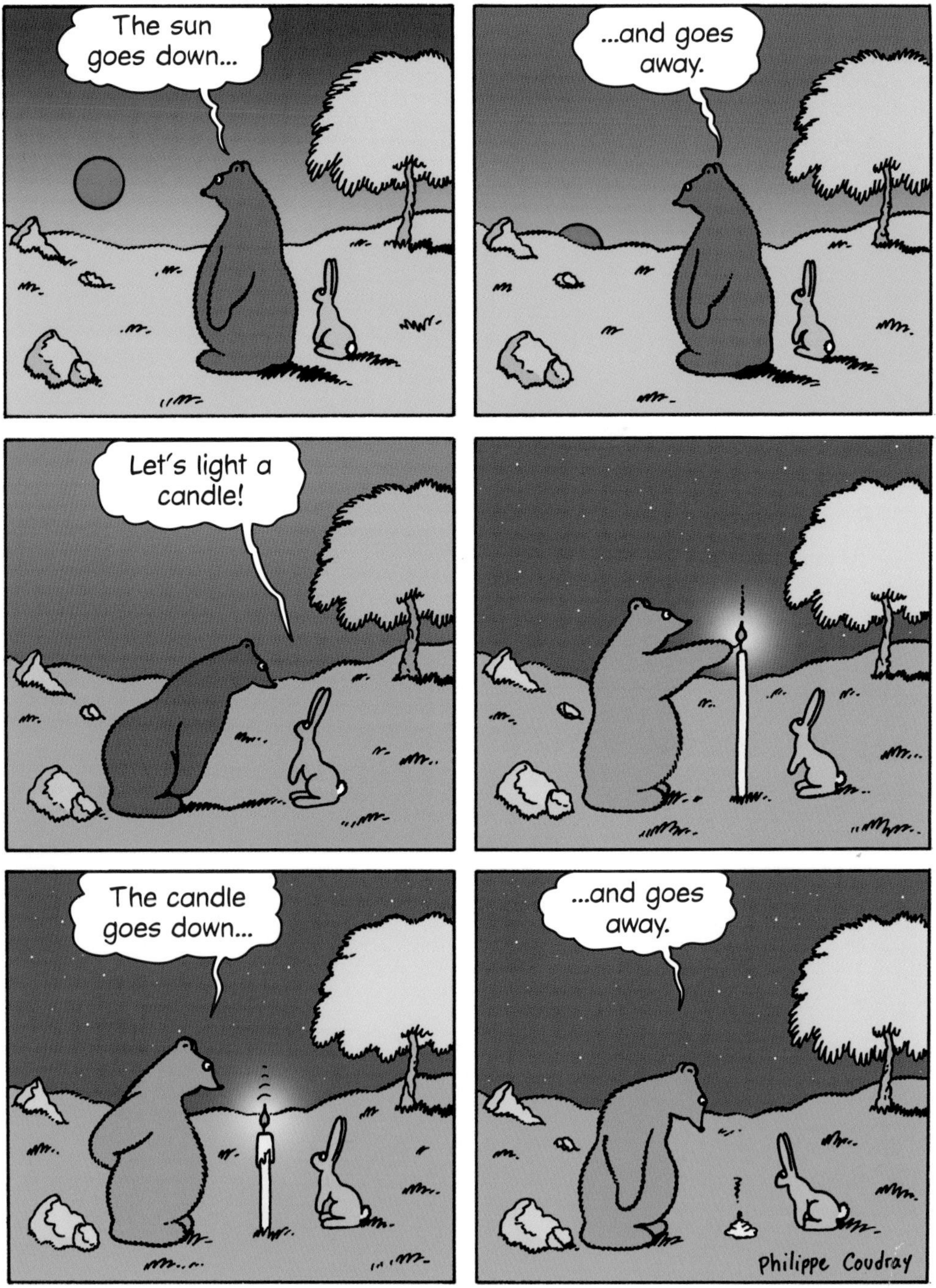
The sun goes down...
...and goes away.
Let's light a candle!
The candle goes down...
...and goes away.
Philippe Coudray

Winter is coming

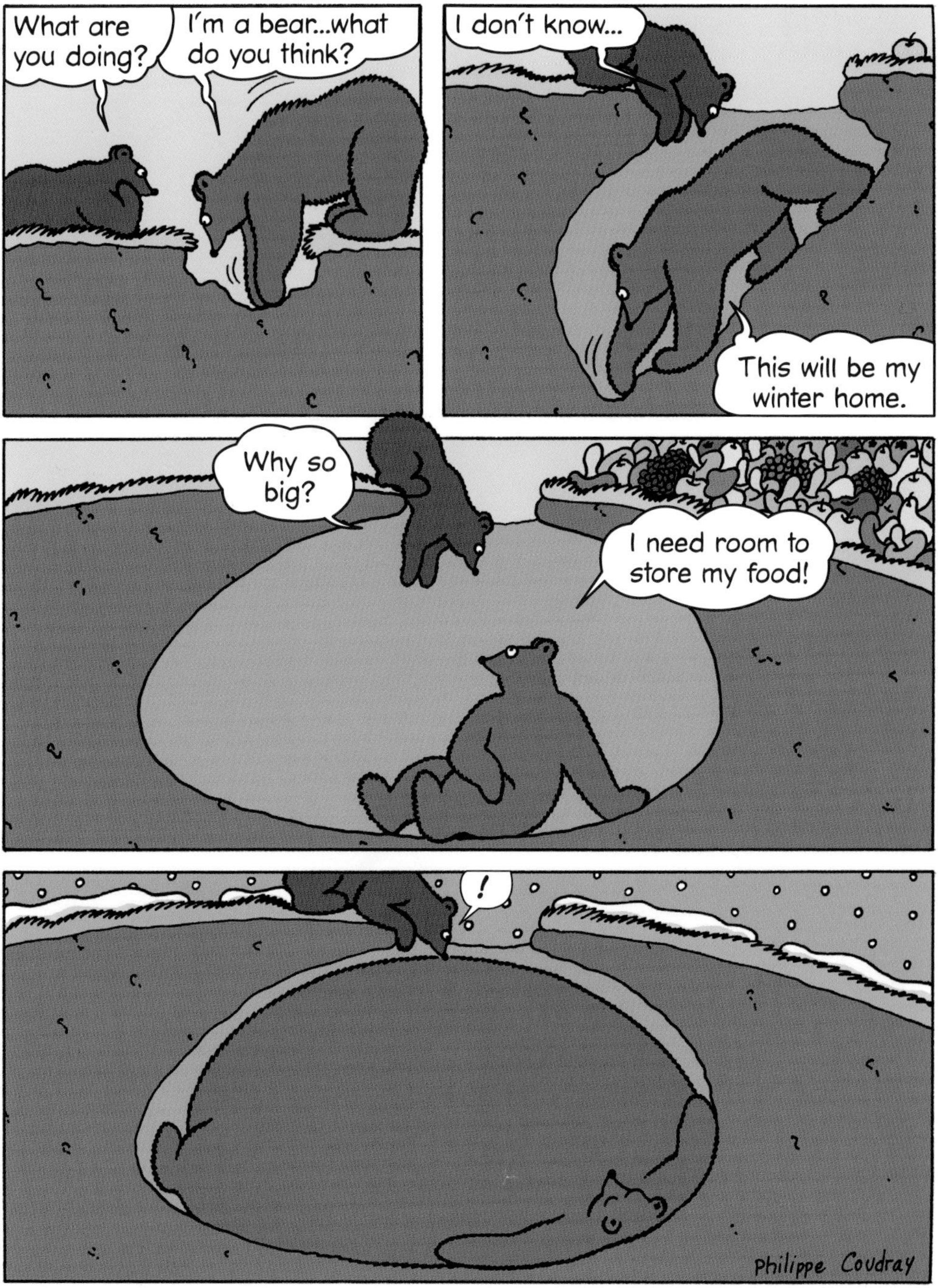
What are you doing?
I'm a bear...what do you think?
I don't know...
This will be my winter home.
Why so big?
I need room to store my food!
!
Philippe Coudray

Too much wind!

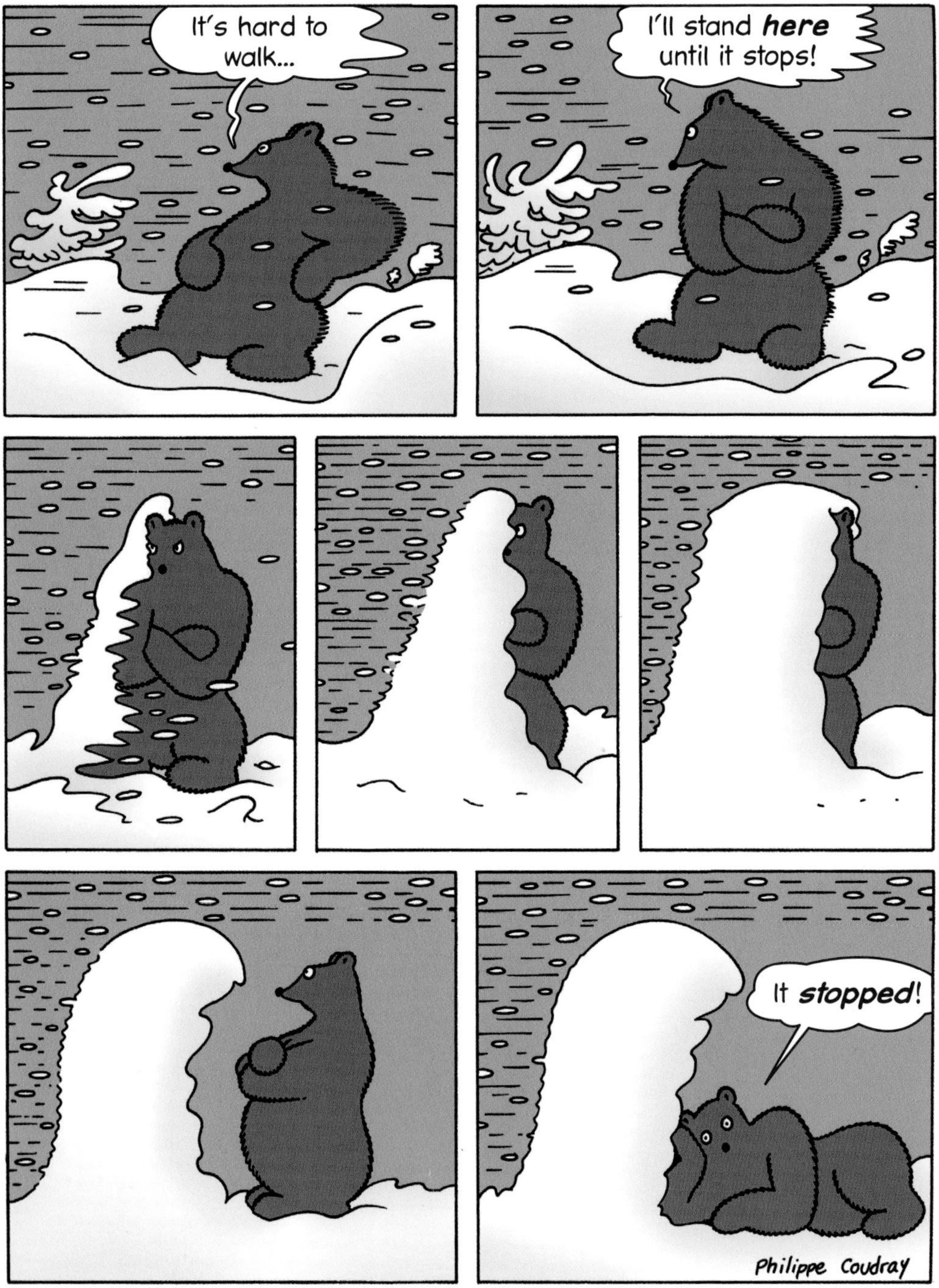
It's hard to walk...
I'll stand **here** until it stops!
It **stopped**!
Philippe Coudray

The winner

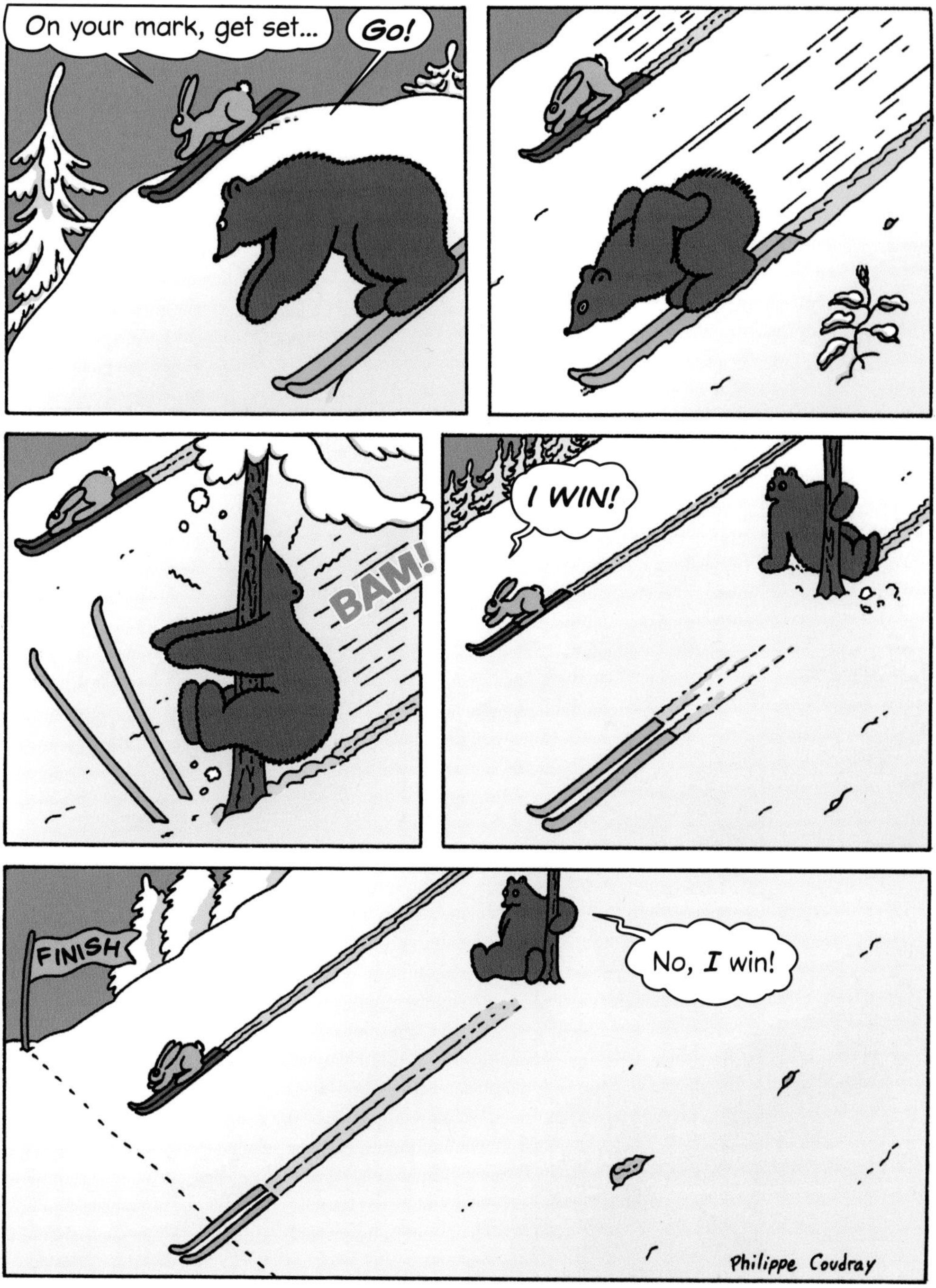
On your mark, get set...
Go!
BAM!
I WIN!
FINISH
No, I win!
Philippe Coudray

A good friend

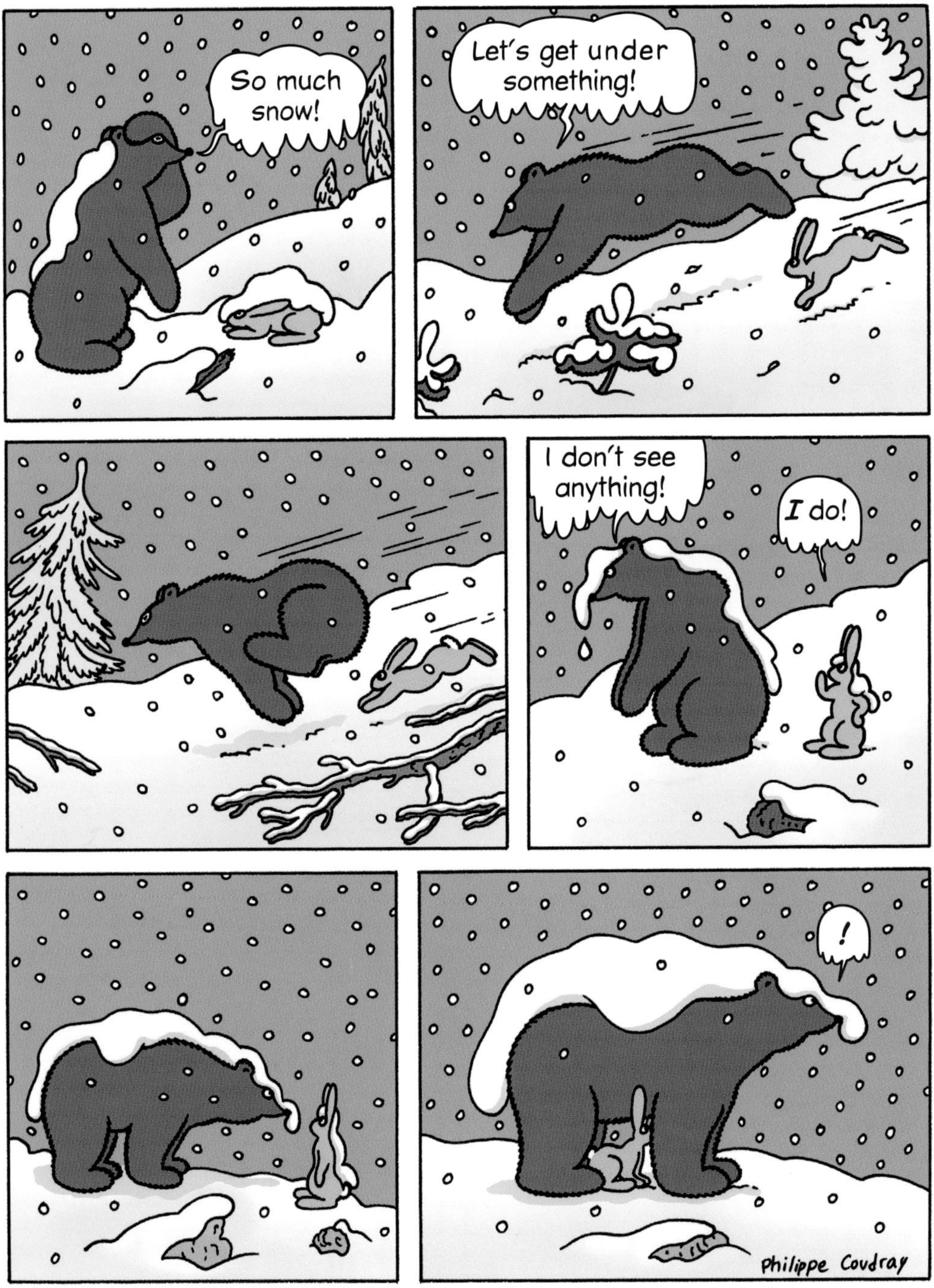
So much snow!
Let's get under something!
I don't see anything!
I do!
!
Philippe Coudray

Do as you are told!

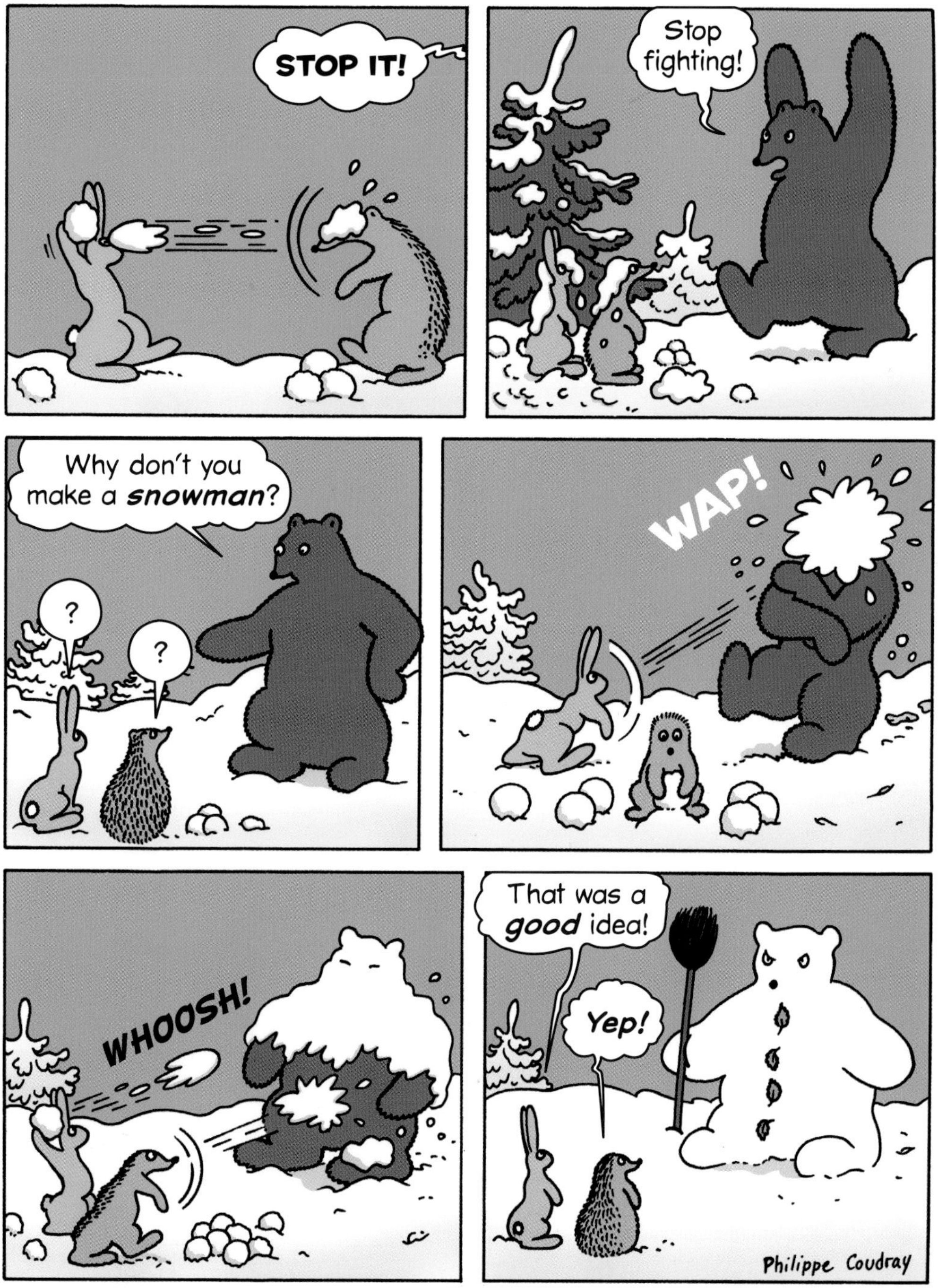
STOP IT!
Stop fighting!
Why don't you make a *snowman*?
?
?
WAP!
WHOOSH!
That was a *good* idea!
Yep!
Philippe Coudray

Friends

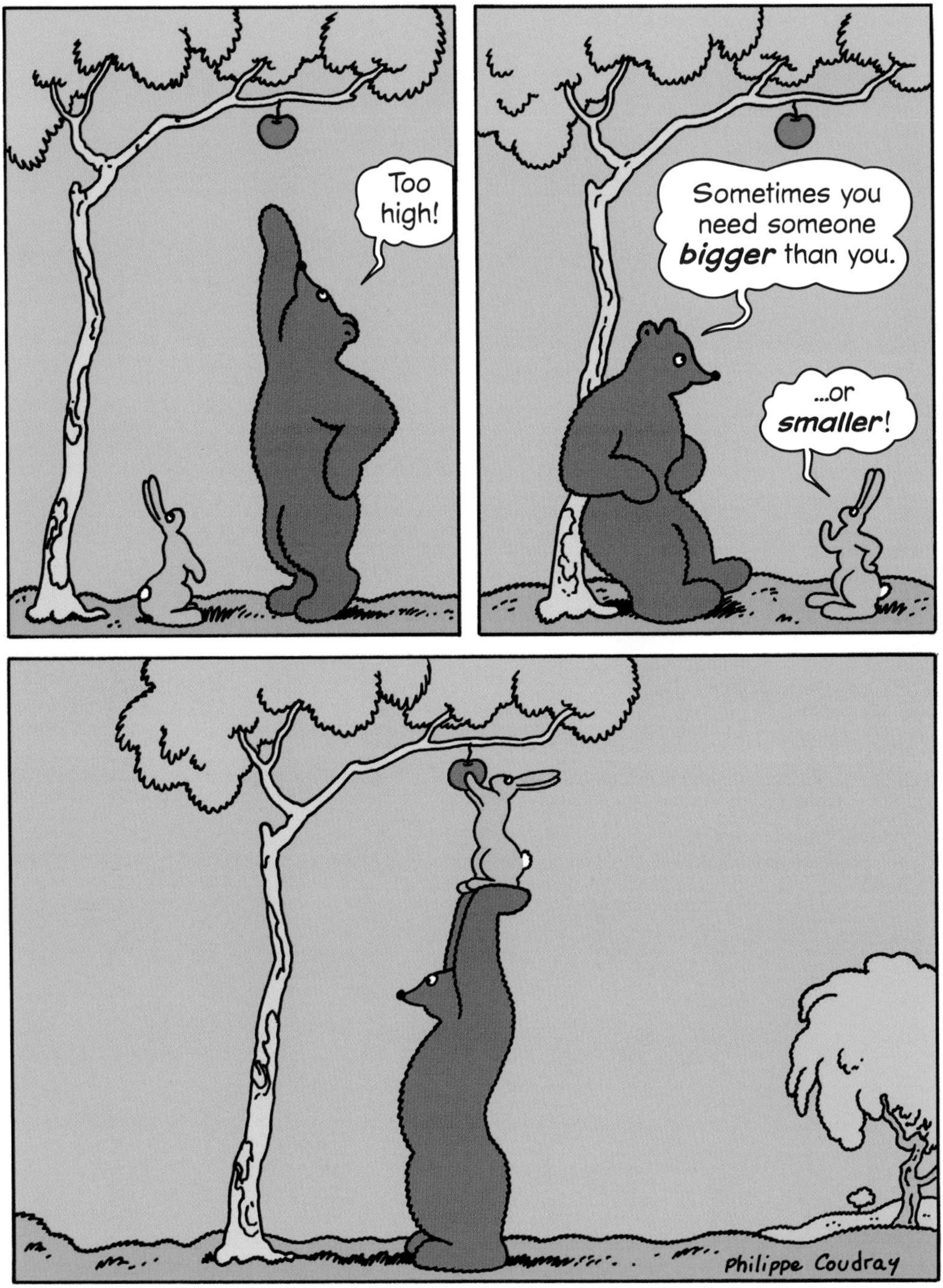
Too high!
Sometimes you need someone **bigger** than you.
...or **smaller**!
Philippe Coudray

The biggest fish

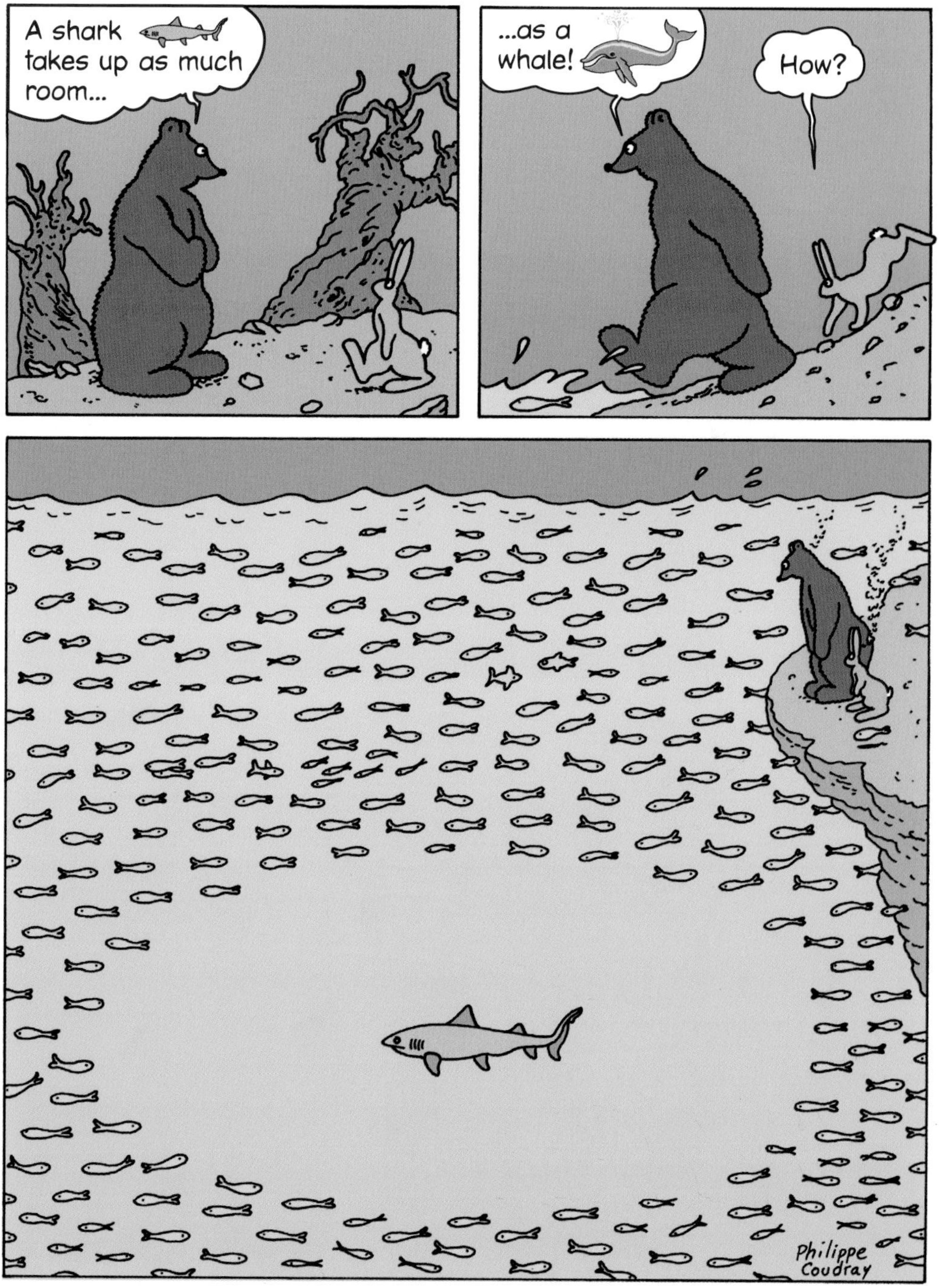
A shark takes up as much room...
...as a whale!
How?
Philippe Coudray

I want to play!

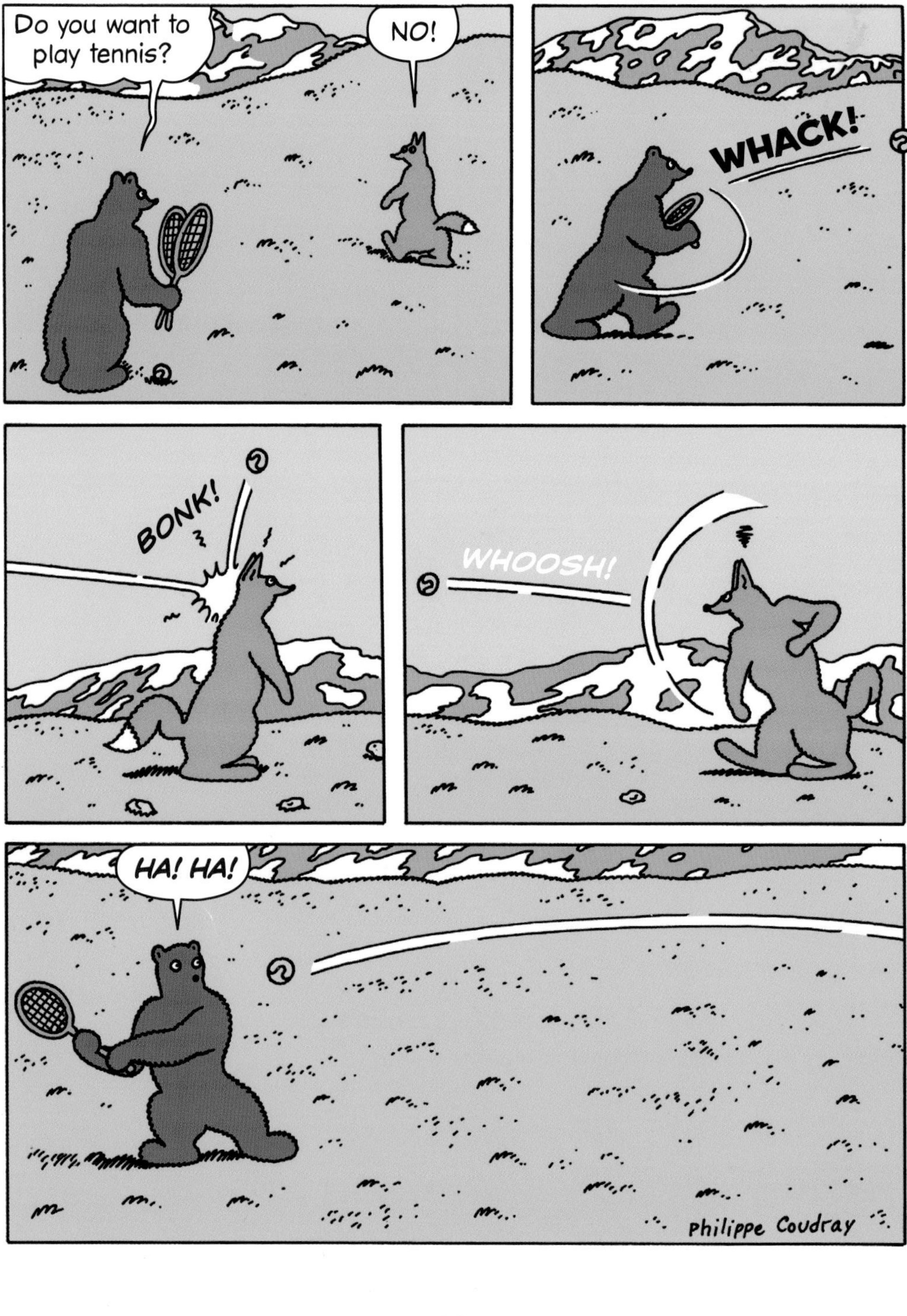
Do you want to play tennis?
NO!
WHACK!
BONK!
WHOOSH!
HA! HA!
Philippe Coudray

The hot dog

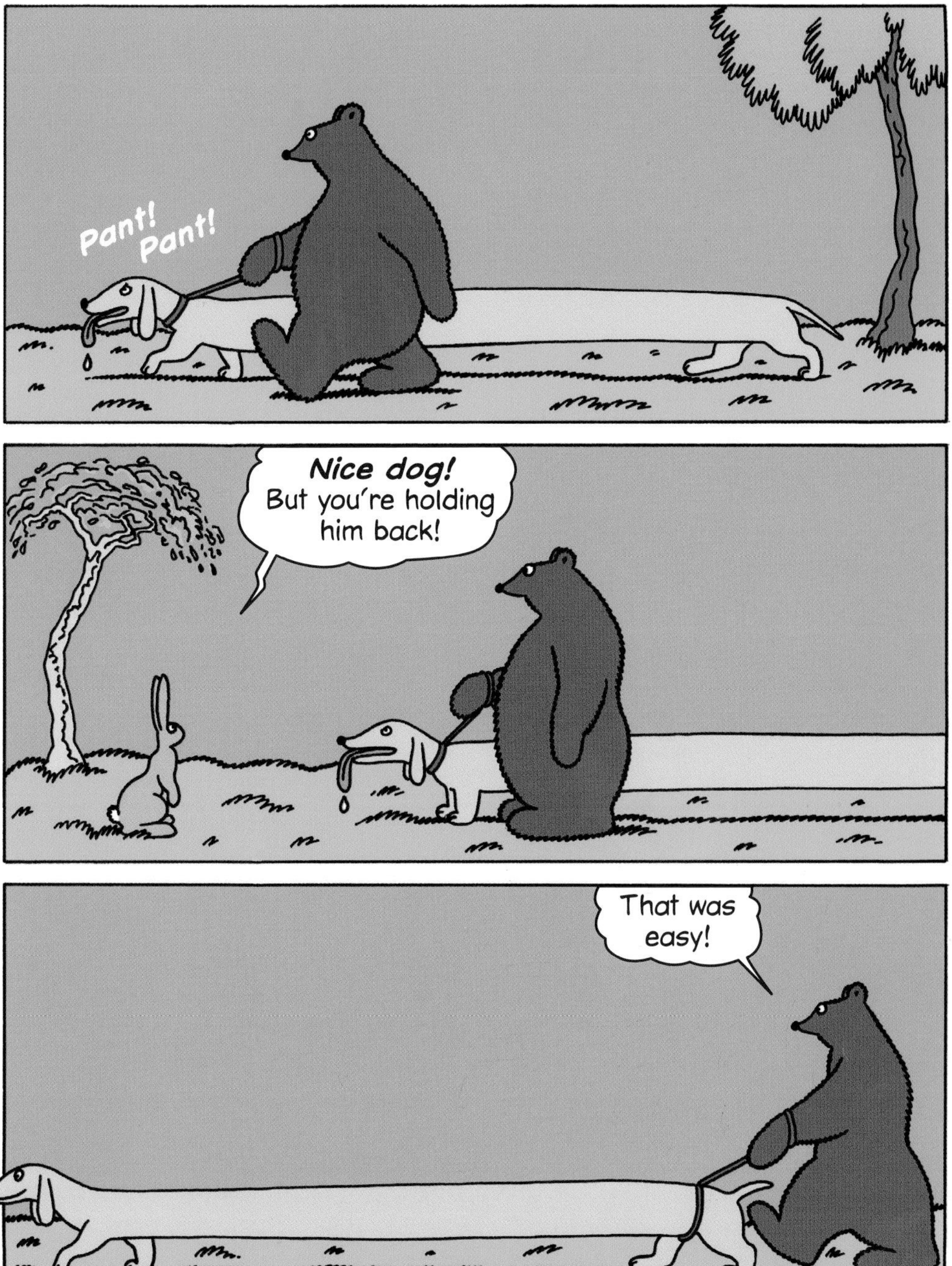
Pant! Pant!
Nice dog! But you're holding him back!
That was easy!
Philippe Coudray

Back to school

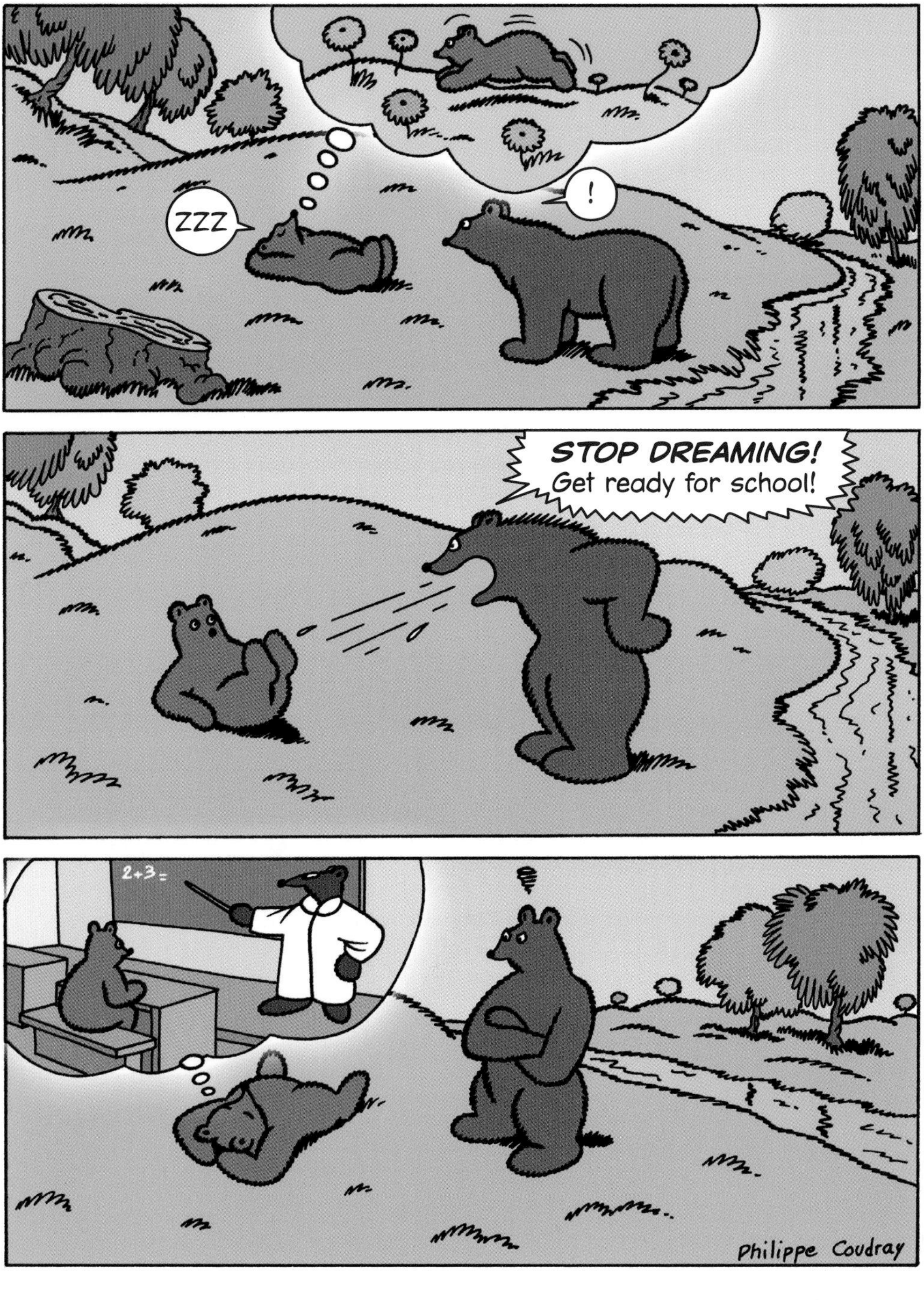
ZZZ
!
STOP DREAMING!
Get ready for school!
2+3=
Philippe Coudray

The comic strip

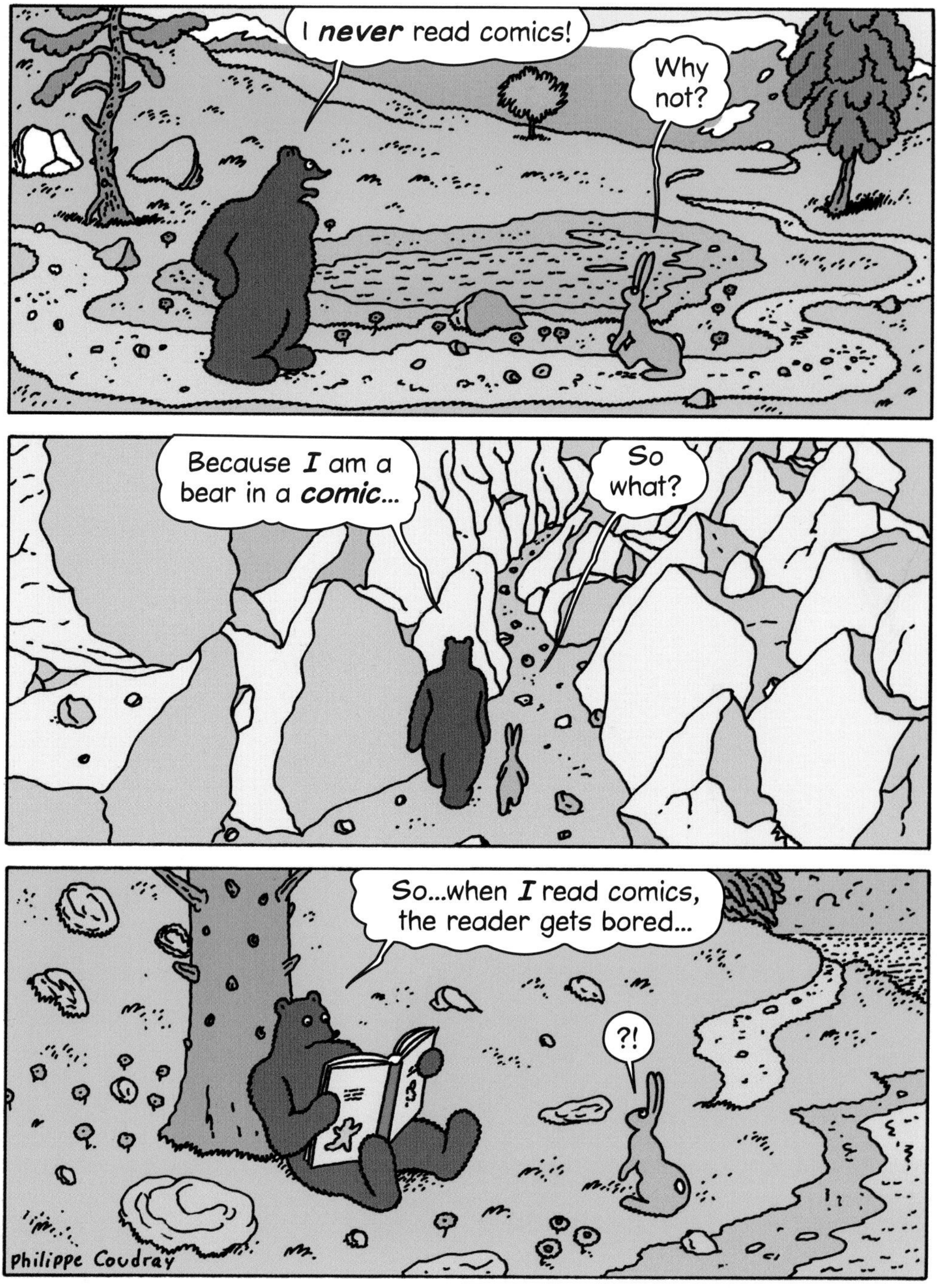
I **never** read comics!
Why not?
Because **I** am a bear in a **comic**...
So what?
So...when **I** read comics, the reader gets bored...
?!
Philippe Coudray

THE END

ABOUT THE AUTHOR

PHILIPPE COUDRAY loves drawing comics, and his many children's books are often used in the schools of France, his home country. In fact, his work was chosen by students to win the prestigious Angoulême Prix des Écoles. Philippe's twin brother Jean-Luc is also a humorist, and they relish any opportunity to collaborate on children's books and comics. Although he lives in Bordeaux, Philippe does not especially like wine. He does enjoy painting, creating stereoscopic images, and traveling to Canada, where he looks for Bigfoot. Though he continues to search each year, Benjamin Bear will always be his favorite wild animal.

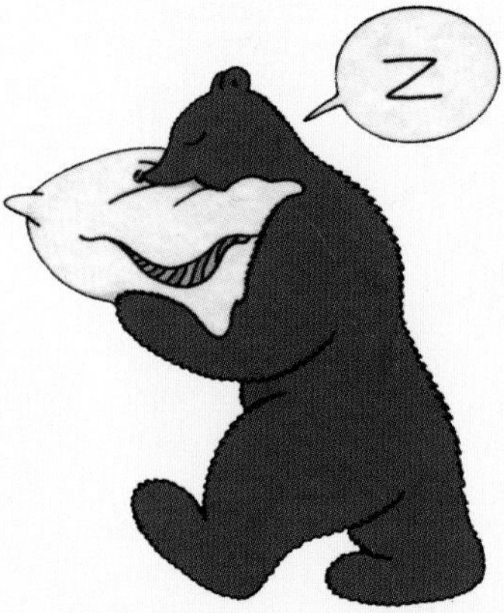
Z

HOW TO READ
COMICS WITH KIDS

Kids **love** comics! They are naturally drawn to the details in the pictures, which make them want to read the words. Comics beg for repeated readings and let both emerging and reluctant readers enjoy complex stories with a rich vocabulary. But since comics have their own grammar, here are a few tips for reading them with kids:

GUIDE YOUNG READERS: Use your finger to show your place in the text, but keep it at the bottom of the speaking character so it doesn't hide the very important facial expressions.

HAM IT UP! Think of the comic book story as a play and don't hesitate to read with expression and intonation. Assign parts or get kids to supply the sound effects, a great way to reinforce phonics skills.

LET THEM GUESS. Comics provide lots of context for the words, so emerging readers can make informed guesses. Like jigsaw puzzles, comics ask readers to make connections, so check a young audience's understanding by asking "What's this character thinking?" (but don't be surprised if a kid finds some of the comics' subtle details faster than you).

TALK ABOUT THE PICTURES. Point out how the artist paces the story with pauses (silent panels) or speeded-up action (a burst of short panels). Discuss how the size and shape of the panels carry meaning.

ABOVE ALL, ENJOY! There is of course never one right way to read, so go for the shared pleasure. Once children make the story happen in their imagination, they have discovered the thrill of reading, and you won't be able to stop them. At that point, just go get them more books, and more comics.

www.TOON-BOOKS.com

**SEE OUR FREE ONLINE CARTOON MAKERS,
LESSON PLANS, AND MUCH MORE**

TOON into Reading

LEVEL 1

GRADES K–1

LEXILE BR–100 • GUIDED READING A–G • READING RECOVERY 7–10

FIRST COMICS FOR BRAND-NEW READERS

- 200–300 easy sight words
- short sentences
- often one character
- single time frame or theme
- 1–2 panels per page

LEVEL 2

GRADES 1–2

LEXILE BR–170 • GUIDED READING G–J • READING RECOVERY 11–17

EASY-TO-READ COMICS FOR EMERGING READERS

- 300–600 words
- short sentences and repetition
- story arc with few characters in a small world
- 1–4 panels per page

LEVEL 3

GRADES 2–3

LEXILE 150–300 • GUIDED READING J–N • READING RECOVERY 17–19

CHAPTER-BOOK COMICS FOR ADVANCED BEGINNERS

- 800–1000+ words in long sentences
- broad world as well as shifts in time and place
- long story divided in chapters
- reader needs to make connections and speculate

COLLECT THEM ALL!

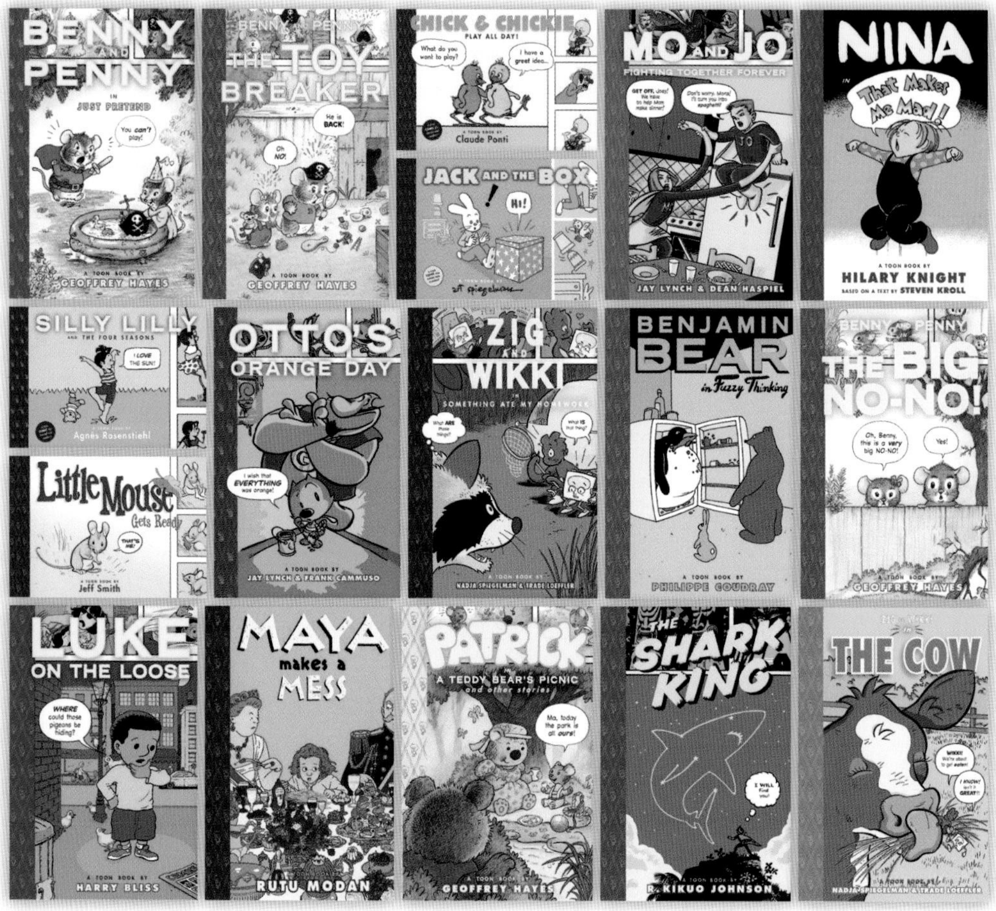
BENNY AND PENNY IN JUST PRETEND
You can't play!
A TOON BOOK BY GEOFFREY HAYES
BENNY AND PENNY IN THE TOY BREAKER
He is BACK!
Oh NO!
A TOON BOOK BY GEOFFREY HAYES
CHICK & CHICKIE PLAY ALL DAY!
What do you want to play?
I have a great idea...
A TOON BOOK BY Claude Ponti
JACK AND THE BOX
HI!
MO AND JO FIGHTING TOGETHER FOREVER
JAY LYNCH & DEAN HASPIEL
NINA IN That Makes Me Mad!
A TOON BOOK BY HILARY KNIGHT
BASED ON A TEXT BY STEVEN KROLL
SILLY LILLY AND THE FOUR SEASONS
I LOVE THE SUN!
Agnès Rosenstiehl
Little Mouse Gets Ready
Jeff Smith
OTTO'S ORANGE DAY
I wish that EVERYTHING was orange!
A TOON BOOK BY JAY LYNCH & FRANK CAMMUSO
ZIG AND WIKKI IN SOMETHING ATE MY HOMEWORK
A TOON BOOK BY NADJA SPIEGELMAN & TRADE LOEFFLER
BENJAMIN BEAR in Fuzzy Thinking
A TOON BOOK BY PHILIPPE COUDRAY
BENNY AND PENNY IN THE BIG NO-NO!
Oh, Benny, this is a very big NO-NO!
Yes!
A TOON BOOK BY GEOFFREY HAYES
LUKE ON THE LOOSE
WHERE could those pigeons be hiding?
A TOON BOOK BY HARRY BLISS
MAYA makes a MESS
RUTU MODAN
PATRICK IN A TEDDY BEAR'S PICNIC and other stories
Ma, today the park is all ours!
A TOON BOOK BY GEOFFREY HAYES
THE SHARK KING
I WILL find you!
A TOON BOOK BY R. KIKUO JOHNSON
THE COW
A TOON BOOK BY NADJA SPIEGELMAN & TRADE LOEFFLER

TOON BOOKS SET 1

Set of 10 hardcover books	978-1-61479-298-7
Benny and Penny in Just Pretend	978-1-61479-148-5
Benny and Penny in the Toy Breaker	978-1-61479-149-2
Chick & Chickie Play All Day!	978-1-61479-150-8
Jack and the Box	978-1-61479-151-5
Mo and Jo Fighting Together Forever	978-1-61479-152-2
Nina in That Makes Me Mad!	978-1-61479-153-9
Otto's Orange Day	978-1-61479-154-6
Silly Lilly and the Four Seasons	978-1-61479-155-3
Silly Lilly in What Will I Be Today?	978-1-61479-156-0
Zig and Wikki in Something Ate My Homework	978-1-61479-157-7

TOON BOOKS SET 2

Set of 8 hardcover books	978-1-61479-298-7
Benjamin Bear in Fuzzy Thinking	978-1-61479-299-4
Benny and Penny in the Big No-No!	978-1-61479-300-7
Little Mouse Gets Ready	978-1-61479-301-4
Luke on the Loose	978-1-61479-302-1
Maya Makes a Mess	978-1-61479-303-8
Patrick in a Teddy Bear's Picnic and Other Stories	978-1-61479-304-5
The Shark King	978-1-61479-305-2
Zig and Wikki in the Cow	978-1-61479-306-9

Easy Books

94 Coudray, Philippe.

Benjamin Bear in
Fuzzy thinking.

DATE			